Tumble
& Blue

Tumble & Blue

CASSIE BEASLEY

Dial Books for Young Readers

DIAL BOOKS FOR YOUNG READERS
PENGUIN YOUNG READERS GROUP

An imprint of Penguin Random House LLC
375 Hudson Street, New York, NY 10014

Library of Congress Cataloging-in-Publication Data
Names: Beasley, Cassie, author.
Title: Tumble and Blue / Cassie Beasley.
Description: New York : Dial Books for Young Readers, [2017] | Summary: In order for Tumble Wilson and Blue Montgomery to fix their ancestors' mistakes and banish the bad luck that has followed them around for all of their lives, they must face Munch, the mysterious golden alligator who cast the curse centuries ago. | Identifiers: LCCN 2016040458| ISBN 9780525428442 (hardcover) | ISBN 9780698189072 (ebook) | Subjects: | CYAC: Luck—Fiction. | Blessing and cursing—Fiction. | Friendship—Fiction. | Alligators—Fiction. Classification: LCC PZ7.1.B432 Tu 2017 | DDC [Fic]—dc23 | LC record available at https://lccn.loc.gov/2016040458

Printed in the United States of America • 10 9 8 7 6 5 4 3 2 1

Design by Jason Henry | Text set in Adobe Caslon Pro

For my sister, Kate.
Thank you for sharing your
adventures with me. Thank
you for coming along on mine.
Let's keep being us.

Tumble
& Blue

From time to time, I bother to notice them.

Tourists. They come reeking of their bug repellents and their sunscreens, and the *clicker-snap* of their cameras nibbles away at the song of the swamp until I wonder if they can hear it at all.

In my memory, the humans who traveled the Okefenokee were a different sort. These new ones are less afraid. More curious. And, on the whole, they are quite a bit plumper.

It would be a lie to say I have not felt the stirrings of temptation. Especially in the deep summer, when the sun glazes them with sweat so that they glisten, juicy and bright as silver fish.

Scrumptious, but I resist. My business with mankind is not, strictly speaking, that of the predator.

I do have to remind myself of that when they come carrying maps. How they love those little guides with their safe paths through the swamp, all dotted out and color-coded. Acres of prairie and blackwater and cypress and pine captured as lines on bits of paper. Made small as gnats.

Such arrogant morsels, you humans. That's something that hasn't changed.

Which brings me to the beginning, to a couple of humans long dead but still causing trouble for their descendants. Almira LaFayette, Walcott Montgomery—names from a story that is only now approaching its end.

It's been two hundred years, and I still remember the taste of them on the night air. Thick, greedy, sweet with desperation. When they met on the edge of the swamp, the red sickle moon was cutting a hole in the black of the sky.

My moon.

And in its bloody light those two bad people were looking for an easy way out of the messes they'd made. Montgomery was a horse thief. LaFayette was a murderous young bride. He had robbed a militiaman, and she had shot her husband in the gut with a revolver three days after the wedding.

Why?

Perhaps they had their reasons. I didn't care to ask. What matters is that they ran from justice and toward me, and they reached my island at the same time.

Precisely the same time. An irksome situation for me and a tricky one for them.

I offer only one change of fate. Only one chance at a new future. Those are the rules, and they can be terribly sharp when broken.

Well. At least they didn't use maps to find me. Even Montgomery and LaFayette knew that much.

Creatures like me don't fit in between a cartographer's lines.

Creatures like me . . .

We can only be found in the places where maps dare not go.

ONE

BLUE

B lue Montgomery almost missed the sign. Kudzu was
vining up its wooden posts, and its paint had begun
to peel. It looked more like part of the wilderness around
it than something made by human hands.

But his dad seemed to know where the turn was even
in the dark. He steered the truck off the asphalt and onto
dirt, and in the shine of the headlights, Blue had just
enough time to read, WELCOME TO MURKY BRANCH, GA.
and, POPULATION: 339.

"'Bout two miles to your granny's house from here!"
Alan Montgomery raised his voice over the rumble of
the washboard road. "I used to run from our front door
all the way out to the sign. Back when I was your age. I
could make it in under twelve minutes. Not bad at all."

He drummed his fingers on the steering wheel and
gunned the truck's engine.

Blue watched the woods speed by. His dad had been like this ever since they'd left the hotel in Atlanta. Talky. Casual. As if he didn't know that every mile marker they passed stung Blue like a wasp.

There were no more mile markers out here, though. No cell phone reception either. Most of the world had no idea that Murky Branch existed.

The road curved, and through a break in the pines, Blue saw the house. Three stories of ghostly white paint and wraparound porches were illuminated by a moon that was close to full.

"Your granny's going to be so glad to see you," said his dad. "She's been nagging me to bring you around for forever."

He whipped the truck onto the gravel driveway just as the glowing numbers on the dashboard clock changed to read midnight. Rocks flew up to ping against the doors. Blue winced, imagining the scratches and dings in the new paint, but he didn't say anything.

His dad had taken a break from racing last year, but now that he was planning to get back on the track, he only had one speed. Fast.

The truck passed an old chicken coop that was cooping a mower instead of chickens, then a shed with a roll of rusting barbed wire propped against one wall. Blue caught a glimpse of the huge garden beside the house. It was filled with tomato cages, silver pinwheels, and chin-high corn.

His dad dodged a sprinkler, bounced the truck over a coiled hose, and stopped inches from the trunk of a giant pecan tree. "Well," he said, letting go of the wheel, "the place hasn't changed much. You need help getting the—?"

"I've got it," Blue muttered, opening his own door.

Blue's right arm had been in a cast for weeks. He'd tried to stand up to a bully at school and, in hindsight, that hadn't been the best idea. Fighting usually wasn't when you were literally destined to lose.

But the arm would be fine. Sometimes, when the itching let up, Blue forgot that he was wearing the cast at all.

He reached into the truck's backseat, but his dad was already there, stretching to grab the overstuffed duffel bag. "Let me take that for you, Skeeter."

He set off toward the house, and Blue followed, dragging his feet.

The sounds were strange. In Atlanta, even at night, sirens and horns had screamed past the hotel where they'd been living, but here, the darkness was loud with chirring insects and frog song. Blue felt like his ears had been tuned to the wrong channel.

He reached the edge of the porch's wide cement steps and looked up. He had a vague memory of the Montgomery house from when he was a little kid. But it was eerie now and unfamiliar.

Carved over the front door's lintel was a scene that had been painted over so many times the finer details were obscured. Two figures, a man and a woman, were shaking hands under a crescent moon.

The columns that supported the porches were carved as well, some of them into cranes with raised beaks and others into alligators standing on the tips of their tails. The gator nearest Blue had had one of its eyes drilled out. It looked like someone had gouged the creature's soul right out of the socket.

Blue climbed the steps and took in the rest of the porch. A pair of worn-out athletic shoes, dirty with grass clippings, had been left beside the mat. The door had a scuffed bottom and etched windows on either side. He couldn't see through the filmy curtains, but he figured everyone in the house must be asleep.

Thunk.

Blue turned. His dad had dropped the duffel bag onto the porch boards. He was rocking back and forth on his heels like he always did after a long drive.

When he caught Blue's stare, he stopped. "What?"

"Nothing."

Blue bent to pick up the bag with his good hand. He tried to lift it onto his shoulder in one smooth motion, though its weight made his arm burn. He thought he'd managed pretty well, but even in the dark, he could see the way the corners of his dad's eyes creased.

"It's not that heavy," Blue said. "I bet I'm as tough as any of the other cursed Montgomerys."

His dad was looking everywhere but at him. "We've talked about this," he said. "I'm not expecting you to get involved when . . . *if* it happens the way they say it will. You're only here to visit your granny while I work some things out. The timing's a coincidence is all."

Blue wished he would stop lying.

The red moon only appeared once every hundred years. According to family legends, on that night one person could travel into the swamp and claim a great new fate. And when you were cursed—as Blue and half of the other Montgomerys were—a new fate was worth the risk. It couldn't be an accident that his dad had decided to leave him here this summer, when the moon was due to rise again.

"Well," his dad said, scuffing his feet against the mat, "go on in. Your granny hasn't locked a door in seventy years."

"Aren't you going to come in with me? To say hello to everyone?"

His dad just stood there, tall and silent. He was sandy-haired, like Blue, but lately it seemed that was the only thing they had in common. Alan was one of the lucky Montgomerys. One of the gifted ones. He had a talent for winning, and as a racer, he'd been unbeatable.

Blue, on the other hand, couldn't even win a game of tic-tac-toe.

"Nah," his dad said at last. "I've got to be gettin' on."

Blue wondered if they were going to hug each other

good-bye. He kind of wanted to, even though none of this was fair. He took a step forward.

His dad turned away. "Got to be gettin' on," he said again. He stomped down the stairs and paused at the bottom to look back over his shoulder. "Tell your granny I said hello. And your cousins."

"Yessir."

"Don't pay too much attention to anything your granny might say about me. And whatever you do, *don't* tell her I'm taking up racing again. She's got this way of looking at things . . . well, it's soft, that's what, and lord knows you don't need more of that."

Blue stiffened.

His dad was scraping one of his shoes against the patchy grass. "Bye."

Blue didn't reply.

Alan strode back to the pickup. Blue had picked the color. Golden brown. He could see the flecks of glitter in the paint even in the dark.

Blue cleared his throat. "I'll see you soon, right?" he called. "You'll be back by the end of the summer?"

The truck door opened with a *clonk*, and his dad pulled

himself up into the high leather seat. "Just take care of yourself."

"Yes, sir."

But they were supposed to take care of each other.

The door slammed. Blue lifted his cast in a wave, but he was too late. The truck had already taken off across the cluttered yard. Its headlights illuminated the green plastic mailbox at the end of the driveway, and then it was gone.

Blue was alone on the porch of a house he only half remembered, on a night full of sounds that were all wrong.

He stared up at the carving over the door. Once upon a long time ago, one of Blue's ancestors had won the great fate for himself under the red sickle moon. Walcott Montgomery had gone into the Okefenokee Swamp a poor man on the run from his enemies, and he had come out of it different. Luckier.

Wealth, health, long life—Walcott had had it all. And he'd changed the fortunes of every Montgomery who came after him.

If you believed the stories, it wasn't entirely Walcott's

fault that half of the family had ended up cursed. The woman in the carving—Almira LaFayette—had been there, too. She'd made it to the hidden island at the heart of the swamp at the same time as Walcott. They'd fought.

Things had gone wrong.

But it would be someone else's turn this time. And if Blue could be that someone . . .

How, though? Other Montgomerys would be descending on Murky Branch. He assumed it would mostly be the cursed relatives. The famous actors, millionaires, and geniuses didn't need to show up, did they?

But even though the Mongomerys who came might have their own terrible fates to contend with, none of them were born to lose. Spelling bees, video games, hide-and-seek—it didn't matter how simple the competition. Blue couldn't win.

His arm itched and ached inside its cast, and as he scratched at the plaster, he realized how tired he was of being himself.

He looked around the empty porch, and the dirty athletic shoes beside the door pulled at his eyes. None of his own shoes were great for running. He'd only ever been a spectator, and running shoes were for racers. Weren't they?

Weren't they for people like his dad, who was probably halfway back to the highway by now, driving like he was about to cross yet another finish line?

Driving away from Blue.

Thunk.

Blue let the duffel bag fall hard. He kicked off his flip-flops. He stomped over to the shoes.

Racing shoes, he thought. *Not-for-Blue shoes.*

And when he stuffed his bare feet inside of the shoes, they fit. Like they had been waiting for him.

Like they were ready to try something new.

TWO

MORE
TROUBLE

B lue ran down the dirt road, trying to stick to the places where the sand was packed hard and smooth. As he left his grandmother's house beind that night, he stumbled a few times, but his eyes soon adjusted to the moonlight. When he reached the sign, he could read it perfectly.

WELCOME TO MURKY BRANCH, GA, it said. POPULATION: 340.

Blue pulled his cell phone out of his pocket and checked the timer he'd set before starting out. It had taken him a little over sixteen minutes to reach this spot from the house. He'd run as hard as he ever had in his life. He was sweaty all over, and his heart was pumping so hard that he could feel the beat of it in his veins.

But *340.*

The number had been 339 when he and his dad drove

past it. Blue knew it. And he couldn't quite convince himself that someone had shown up to change it in the middle of the night.

He stared at the sign with its choking vines. He felt very sure that he should *do* something about the wrong number. But what did you do about . . . any of this?

Sixteen minutes when his dad used to run the distance in twelve. Being left in a town that wasn't even on maps. A broken arm that was heavy and boiling now inside its cast. Losing in a dozen different ways.

Stop feeling sorry for yourself. Just fix this one thing.

He stood on his tiptoes to scratch at the number on the sign. The paint was old and dry beneath his fingers, but even though it was flaking all over, the 340 refused to peel.

He heard the whoosh of a car in the distance, and he ignored it. He dug his nails in deeper until his fingertips stung. He clawed at the number until his legs started to shake from holding him up.

Finally, Blue dropped back on his heels. "You've got it wrong. I'm just visiting. I'm not part of the population."

The sign didn't say anything.

"I promise," said Blue. "I'll be out of here in no time. So could you change back?"

340.

"Please?" Blue stared at the number until his eyes started to water. Finally, he had to blink.

339.

Blue jumped. *That really just happened,* he thought. *It did.*

He glanced down at the weeds and then back at the sign. The 339 looked so sharp and permanent in the moonlight. Cautiously, Blue reached up with one finger.

"I don't know who you are, but you'd better believe I will find out and tell your parents!"

Blue stumbled and almost fell.

He hadn't heard the car stop behind him, but when he whirled around, he saw that the woman shouting at him was leaning out the window of an old black Thunderbird. He opened his mouth to tell her that his mother hadn't been around since he was a baby and his dad wouldn't care anyway, so good luck tattling to them. But before he could say anything, she was talking again.

"Do you have any idea how late it is? Do you want to

die in a ditch like a darn fool? Get over here! I'm taking you home."

He blinked in the red wash of the taillights and squinted. He took in the woman's curly gray hair and her round face. "Granny Eve?"

"What? You're not one of my—" Blue's grandmother threw open the car door and stepped out.

"Blue Montgomery!" she said. Her stout arms went as limp as her flowery housedress for a second. "Blue! How . . . ? Where did you come from?"

Then she was moving, reaching for him.

"Never mind, never mind! Give me a hug and hop in the car. We've got a situation to deal with."

Blue held a Tupperware cake plate in his lap while the Thunderbird soared through Murky Branch.

"It's not that your daddy didn't mention it at all," Granny Eve was saying. "But that was right after you got into a scrape with that boy at school. Dixon somebody."

"Devon," said Blue.

"That's the name. He called that day, while you were having your arm set, and he said, 'Maybe I'll bring Blue by to visit sometime. It's been too long.' And I said, 'That'll be nice, Alan. Maybe you could stay awhile, too.' And he said, 'I'll think about it.'"

"Oh."

"I'm perfectly happy to have you!" Granny Eve said hastily. "Delighted. Excited. I just wasn't expecting you tonight."

"I'm excited to be here, too." Blue didn't know what he was feeling, but it wasn't excitement. It was something squirming and heavy. His dad hadn't even called to warn his grandmother.

He'd *dumped* Blue.

"You can toss that plate into the back," said Granny Eve. "I've been meaning to return it to Goat Flat. He baked me an Italian cream cake two weeks ago."

Blue dropped the Tupperware behind his seat, but when he turned back around, he wished he'd kept it. His hands suddenly didn't know what to do. He blinked down at his cast.

Granny Eve cleared her throat before an awkward silence could creep into the car. "You're awfully sweaty," she said. "Turn on the air. I don't know what you were thinking, running around at midnight like some vampire hoodlum. Why didn't your daddy bring you into the house like a normal person? That's what I want to know."

"It wasn't my fault." Blue reached for the air conditioner.

"Of course it wasn't! Alan's a grown man, and I raised him to behave better than that."

"No," said Blue. "I mean . . . the fight at school. It wasn't my fault. Did Dad say that it was?"

The idea bothered him almost as much as the fact that he'd been left.

"Well, he's not very talkative. Not with me. I think he just said, 'Blue got into a scuffle,' or something along those lines."

"It wasn't a *scuffle*. Dad told me I should stand up for myself," said Blue. "He said it was the only way to get Devon to stop messing with me all the time. He said I had to stop being a . . . a doormat."

Doormat, doormat, doormat, thought Blue. It was something you scraped mud off on. Something everyone stomped all over.

"I swear," said Granny Eve, "sometimes Alan doesn't

have the sense God gave a goose. Did he forget that you couldn't *win* a fight?"

"I was only trying to do what he wanted," said Blue. "Devon was going to take my field trip money."

Blue had hated it so much. The bullying. Devon had chosen to pick on him for no reason he could fathom, and then, when he started demanding that Blue pay him off to be left alone . . . Blue hadn't known how to make it stop, but he had been willing to try anything.

"Well, someone obviously needed to give him a talking to, but you were *not* that someone. No fighting while you're living with me."

"I'm not stupid," said Blue.

"I'm not worried about your brains, honey, I'm worried about your health. We don't go asking for *more* trouble in this family."

She steered the car down an azalea-lined driveway.

"Well," she muttered as they approached the large brick house at the end of the drive, "at least *some* of us don't."

They parked on the edge of the front lawn, and Blue frowned at the scene before them. Someone was standing behind an azalea bush, pointing the beam of a flashlight up at a dark figure on the roof of the house. Something like confetti was drifting through the air as the figure spun in circles and waved its arms.

"What is this place?"

"It's the Okra Lane Home for Seniors."

"Somebody's twirling around on the roof."

"Yes." Granny Eve sighed. "That's your great-grand-mother."

THREE

MA MYRTLE

Murky Branch had two churches, a gas station with three pumps, and a tiny hardware store that also sold bait and tackle. The largest and most successful business in the area was a restaurant called Flat's, which was known for its "Universally Adored Swamp Cakes." These were pancakes, but green. The universal adoration was somewhat in doubt.

You could see the whole town from the rooftop of the Okra Lane Home for Seniors. And if the wind was right, you could catch a whiff of cooking grease from Flat's.

Not that many people were in the habit of standing on Okra Lane's roof.

It was meant to be a quiet place, tucked away from the street behind a tangle of overgrown azalea beds. Most of the residents had seen their eightieth birthdays come and go, and they were less than interested in shimmying up the shingles.

This suited Myrtle Montgomery just fine.

Ma Myrtle—that was what most folks called her regardless of whether or not she was their Ma—had an affection for doing what others thought she shouldn't. On the night Blue arrived in Murky Branch, the Okra Lane staff thought she shouldn't be out on the roof. And no doubt the other Montgomerys, if she had asked them, would have thought she shouldn't be tearing pages out of a certain, very important, family history book that had been locked away for decades.

But that was what she was doing.

Ma Myrtle stood on the roof in her nightdress, slippers slipping against the eaves, and she ripped out one page after another. She shredded them with her bony fingers and tossed the pieces into the air.

All the details about Walcott Montgomery's trip into the swamp drifted away like dandelion seeds.

By the time Eve and Blue arrived on the scene, the book was half as thick as it had been. Ma Myrtle lifted it over her head in both hands and spun in a circle.

"How do you like *that*?" she said to the moon. "Who's in control of the story now, you old rock? Who's going to have the last laugh this time round?"

The moon wasn't in the habit of answering Ma Myrtle, but she laughed all the same.

Eve Montgomery took stock of the situation on the roof and sent Blue to help the owner of Okra Lane fetch a ladder.

After he'd left, she called up to her mother. "Ma Myrtle, what do you think you're doing up on that roof? You're scaring the daylights out of poor Mrs. Lane."

Ma Myrtle squinted down at her. "Eve! My little Evie. Hello, young thing. Isn't it a wondrous night?"

Eve's hands went to her hips. "It was wondrous until they called me out here, Mama. Sit down and we'll send someone up to get you."

"Nonsense, Evie. You know how I hate to be fetched."

"What's that in your hand? They said you were tossing down pieces of paper."

Ma Myrtle stretched herself taller. "They'll be coming

here," she said. "Every one of them thinking the new fate belongs to them."

"The other Montgomerys?" said Eve. "Of course they will, but that's got nothing to do with us."

"It does now!" Ma Myrtle announced. "I'm taking matters in hand. Our family missed the last red moon, you know. One hundred years ago they were too busy fighting among themselves. They *wasted* their chance, and nobody ever made it to the alligator. Not. This. Time."

She punctuated each word by swinging the book like a judge's gavel.

Eve groaned. "Mama, that's not . . . that had better not be the family history."

"It's my book," Ma Myrtle retorted. "Because I'm the oldest. I decide who reads the story, and I've decided that nobody reads it but me."

"Did you at least memorize the pages before you ripped them out?"

"I'm not crazy!" said Ma Myrtle. "Now step aside. I'm coming down."

"Mrs. Lane and Blue went to get a ladder."

"Blue?"

"Alan's left him here."

"Aha! It's already started. He's after the great fate!"

"No, he's just here."

"Is he?" said Ma Myrtle. "Maybe so, with his curse. At any rate, he won't be much good for what I've got planned."

"Lord help us."

"Nobody's going to muddle it up this time, you hear? It's going to be a worthy Montgomery who heads into that swamp. I'm going to choose the person myself."

"We'll talk about it."

"I've already talked about it with the moon. Step aside."

Eve looked over her shoulder. "Here they come with the ladder."

"Ladders are for people who don't know what I know," said Ma Myrtle. She shook her head so that her wispy white hair flew.

"And what do you think you know?"

"I know," said Ma Myrtle, throwing her shoulders back, "when I'm going to die."

Eve froze. "You mean . . ."

"My talent!" said Ma Myrtle proudly. "I've finally managed to see my own end."

"*Mama.*"

"And it's not tonight!"

So saying, Myrtle Montgomery stepped cat-light across the roof and right over the edge.

Blue shouted and dropped the ladder he'd been dragging.

Eve shouted and launched herself toward the house.

Mrs. Lane didn't make a sound, but she collapsed like her bones had been jellied. She and Ma Myrtle hit the ground at the same time.

By all rights, Ma Myrtle should have been flattened like a swamp cake. But she was a Montgomery, and one of the lucky ones besides. Her talent was predicting the end of things. She never had to check the oven timer to know when supper was going to be done. And, grim as it was, she never had to check with a doctor to know when *people* were going to be done. She'd been making a nuisance of herself at Okra Lane by forecasting the expiration dates of her fellow residents, who hardly ever appreciated it.

And now she was armed and armored with the time of her own death. That was what had prompted her to scale the roof in the first place, and perhaps it was what made her land *just so* in Okra Lane's fluffiest azalea bush. She rolled out of the shrub to face Eve, who still had her hands stretched out as though to catch something.

"Gracious," Ma Myrtle said, picking twigs out of her hair, "that was the most exhilarating thing I've done in twenty years!"

"Mama," Eve said. "You're going to . . . are you sure you . . . ?"

Ma Myrtle beamed and spread her arms wide. "I'm going to die in exactly thirty-seven days! And let me tell you, I am not going to waste an instant between now and then!"

I didn't much approve of Walcott's little book.

It was a map, of sorts, disguised as a story, and it was never meant to last.

The Montgomerys who would soon be flocking to Murky Branch were hungry for details. They wanted to know when and how and where. They wanted an instruction manual.

But Ma Myrtle, clever reptile, had wrapped her jaws around it first.

Without the book, they would have only what they were meant to have. The legend.

A red crescent moon, the sharp bite of fate.

And me.

FOUR

WELCOME TO
THE ATTIC

Blue spent most of his first day in Murky Branch trying to figure out how he fit into his own family. Three of his cousins lived with his grandmother.

The twins, Jenna and Ida, were sixteen. They were willowy and pale, and they would have been identical down to the last eyelash if Ida hadn't chopped her blond hair short and dyed it with rainbow stripes.

Jenna had the ability to charm any animal she met, which was a useful talent when it came to protecting her twin. Animals hated Ida. The chicken coop in front of the house was empty, they told Blue, because Ida had almost lost an eye to an enraged Rhode Island Red.

Then there was Howard who, at fourteen, was two years older than Blue, and gifted with the weirdest skill Blue had ever heard of. "I'm good at eating," he explained that morning while Blue waited for his chance to dip from a pan of scrambled eggs on the stove.

As he spoke, Howard was shoveling a quivering pile of eggs onto his plate beside a leaning tower of tomato slices. He didn't look anything like the twins. Or like Blue for that matter. All of Eve Montgomery's grandchildren had different grandfathers, and it showed. Howard had dark hair and black eyes, and he was so muscular that Blue was sure he'd never had to deal with being picked on at a school.

"How is *eating* a talent?" he asked.

Howard scooped a forkful of egg into his mouth and gulped.

"I can eat as much as I want," he said, gesturing to the plate, "without making myself sick or needing to burn off the calories."

He pulled up the sleeves of his ratty black T-shirt and struck a cartoonish pose in front of the stove, flexing his biceps so that the veins in his arms stood out. "See? I could totally arm wrestle you to the ground."

Blue snorted and started scraping the last bits of egg

out of the pan. "*Everyone* can arm wrestle me to the ground. Even when one of my arms isn't broken."

"True," said Howard cheerfully. "But you didn't steal *everyone*'s nasty old shoes off the porch. Did you forget to pack your own or something?"

They sat down at the table with the twins, who were drinking huge mugs of coffee. Blue was about to start quizzing Howard on how, exactly, his gift worked— could he survive on candy bars and chips? Did he ever get full? But Ma Myrtle shuffled into the kitchen and everything went downhill fast.

She spied Howard's mountain of eggs, and in a moment the two of them were embroiled in what Blue guessed was an ongoing argument. Ma Myrtle wanted Howard to challenge someone named Bagget Flat to an eatathon.

"I've *told* you," Howard said irritably, "I don't want to do eating contests. Not even against the Flats. It's not fair."

"Nonsense," she said. "Unfair is Bagget Flat giving me food poisoning last Easter. He knew those deviled eggs had gone bad!"

Ida tucked a strand of pink hair behind her ear. "Ma Myrtle, that was an accident and you know it."

"We Montgomerys have a duty not to squander our talents! We must maintain the family dignity. We—"

"Weren't you up on a roof last night?" Howard retorted. "How dignified is that?"

Jenna sighed and gestured to her sister. Ida nodded. She leaned over to whisper in Blue's ear. "They're just revving up," she said. "This will go on forever. You might as well come upstairs with us if you want a quiet breakfast."

Blue, feeling a little pleased to have been invited, followed the two of them out of the kitchen.

The twins and Howard seemed happy enough to tolerate Blue's presence in the house. Ida was especially friendly, and there was plenty of room to go around. But all too soon, there were other newcomers to the household.

Ma Myrtle spent a lot of time making phone calls to Montgomerys all over the world. She was the only person who knew exactly when the red moon would rise and exactly how to claim the great fate when it did. And she would be the one who decided which member of the family won the chance to change his or her fortune.

Over the next few days, relatives showed up in droves.

Mostly, the arrivals were the ones with bad fates, as Blue had suspected they would be, but others came, too. The empty rooms in the huge old house were filled. Then they were overfilled. Until, at last, an elderly uncle appeared who couldn't climb the house's many staircases, and Blue found himself ousted from his space on the ground floor.

It was five o'clock in the morning, and there wasn't a single empty room to be had.

Blue would have to sleep in the attic.

Ida helped him move his belongings. There was no bed in the attic, but they found an air mattress in a closet. Ida sat on the floor, her pink pajama pants turning gray from all the dust, and tried to figure out how to inflate the mattress while Blue rearranged boxes and ranted about Howard.

"I thought maybe he would share with me! Just his bedroom floor or something. But he wouldn't, and when I tried to force open the door—"

"Ow," Ida said sympathetically.

"Who *electrifies* their doorknob?" Blue kicked a cardboard box. There were dozens of them. He could barely manage to clear a space for the mattress.

"Howard does. Since we were kids. He's not a sharer."

Blue's hand still felt numb from the powerful shock Howard's booby trap had delivered. It didn't improve his mood. "This house is going to fall down if one more cursed person shows up. How many relatives do we even *have*?"

Ida shrugged and leaned back against an old washing machine box. "You know how Montgomerys almost never change our last names. Even people who wouldn't normally count as relations, like our sixth cousins twice removed, are still part of the family."

She set aside the instruction sheet that had come with the mattress. "I think we need a pump of some kind for this."

"Great," Blue grunted, pushing against a heavy crate.

"I know it's a pain," Ida said. "I finally had to move in with Jenna, and we've never shared a bedroom before. Her pets . . ."

"Sorry," Blue said, feeling guilty for complaining. "But she keeps the gerbils in their cages right?"

"Don't call them cages," Ida groaned. "They're 'habitats.' And the little monsters haven't managed to escape. Yet."

Gerbils were the compromise the twins had come up with years ago. Because they were, in theory, safe enough for Ida to be around. But Jenna had trained them. She called them the Gerbellion, and they were smarter, faster, and stronger than normal gerbils.

"It's okay." Ida looked around the attic. "At least there aren't cobwebs in our room."

"Or boxes." Blue's shoulders were starting to ache. The big crate was too heavy to shove. "What's *in* these things anyway?"

"It's . . ." Ida hesitated. "Just junk. Don't bother looking. I'm sure we can find somewhere else to put them when Granny Eve wakes up."

"Not unless she's got another house hidden somewhere. That guy who can hit anything with a slingshot—"

"Great Uncle Morris. Perfect aim."

"Whoever he is, he's sleeping in the *pantry*."

Blue had been introduced to most of the relatives, but remembering their names was impossible. It was easier to think of them as their fates. That cousin who caused car accidents. The aunt who always had a head cold. The semifamous poet. The toddler who sang country music. That guy who had to live outside in a tent because he caught stuff on fire all the time.

"They're everywhere," he said, slumping down on top of the crate.

"Howard says Ma Myrtle has lost her last marble." Ida looked toward the attic's window. It was half hidden behind a stack of storage tubs. "But I think she just wants to distract herself from the fact that she's . . . you know."

Blue did know. "It's still not fair to the rest of you! I mean, this is your house."

"Yours, too, now."

He shook his head. "You know I'm only here for the summer."

"It must be nice." Ida's voice was wistful. "To have a dad who doesn't mind that you weren't born with one of the good fates."

Blue wasn't sure how to answer that. "I thought maybe if I called him and told him how crowded it was here, he might come back early. But I can barely find a moment to use the kitchen phone, and I think that girl who makes the lights flicker fried the one in the foyer."

"Cousin Ernestine—she has electrical issues. But we still have the answering machine," said Ida. "Your dad can leave a message."

Blue had been checking the answering machine three times a day.

"The two of us will just have to stick together until they're all gone in a few weeks," Ida said.

"What?"

"You know." She gestured across the space between them. "We're the only two who can't . . . they're all trying to convince Ma Myrtle she should choose them to make the journey into the swamp and we . . ."

Blue squirmed. As nice as Ida was, he didn't want to be lumped together with her like this.

She didn't seem to notice. "Our school takes a field trip into the Okefenokee almost every year, and I always pretend to have the flu."

Ida's animal problem was no small thing. The same curse had eventually killed their great-great-grandfather.

A plow horse had escaped from its pasture just to have the privilege of trampling him.

"Stomping around in a swamp full of crazed beasts? *No thanks.*" She smiled weakly at Blue. "And you're in the same boat. At least none of the others sees us as a threat. Maybe they'll leave us alone until it's over."

Blue opened his mouth to argue, to say that *he* wasn't going to give up. To tell her that he needed a new fate as much as any of the other Montgomerys did. But Ida leaned toward him and said in a conspiratorial whisper, "Anyway, we've already decided. Howard, Jenna, and I have. *Granny Eve* is the one who should have the new fate. I can't go into the swamp, and Jenna and Howard don't need to."

Blue's stomach flopped inside him like a dying fish.

Granny Eve's fate. He'd *forgotten.* Nobody ever talked about it.

And she'd been so good to him in her own gruff way. Blue had a feeling that a lot of people wouldn't have been as understanding about an estranged grandson showing up on their doorstep with no warning.

"Right." He struggled to hide the upset in his voice.

"Granny Eve. I hadn't thought about . . . but of course if anyone . . . I guess."

Ida nodded. "I know what you're thinking," she said. "Granny Eve isn't *that* old, though. And she's as tough as anyone I know. She could make it through the swamp."

Blue couldn't find an argument.

Granny Eve had practically carried poor Mrs. Lane inside after her fainting spell a few nights ago. And even though Blue had volunteered to do it, she'd climbed onto Okra Lane's roof herself to make sure that there weren't any stray pages from the Montgomery family history to be salvaged.

"She's really tough," he said.

Ida beamed. "Exactly. We're going to make sure she gets the happy ending she deserves. It's the least we can do for her after everything she's done to take care of us. And now that you're here, too . . . well, we're an even stronger team, aren't we?"

Blue's thoughts were so selfish he almost couldn't think them.

"We're going to figure it all out," Ida said confidently. "But for now—"

She stood and reached for a pillowcase-covered bundle she'd carried upstairs with the air mattress. She whipped the pillowcase off to reveal a lopsided Easter basket stuffed with knickknacks. She held it out to Blue.

"Surprise!" she said. "I'm sorry none of it's new, but I haven't really had time to go shopping. I thought you deserved a Welcome to the House present, and this was stuff I had in my room. So . . . welcome to the house. And to the attic, I guess."

Blue examined the contents of the Easter basket.

A rolled-up poster that turned out to be covered in paint splatters. Rainbow-colored, of course.

A tin of breath mints.

A half-burned candle that smelled like lemon cake.

He picked up a picture frame decorated with wooden stars and turned it over in his hands. It was empty. His throat clenched up around an emotion he didn't like at all.

"I didn't bring any . . ."

"Oh, you can use Jenna's printer if you need a photo," said Ida. "She'll pretend to mind, but she won't really."

When Blue didn't answer, her voice turned worried. "I know it's not as good as some of your own stuff. I mean, your dad can buy you whatever you want I guess, but I thought it might be nice to have some things to make the room more homey."

Blue swallowed. "It's great, Ida." He forced a smile and reached into the bottom of the basket. He pulled out a gray plastic box. "I love it. All of it. Even this . . . um . . . this."

"That's a no-kill mousetrap."

"Are there a lot of mice around here?" The attic did seem like the kind of place that would be infested.

"No, it's in case the Gerbellion gerbils ever escape."

Blue laughed, but Ida shook her head. "You've got no idea what they're capable of."

FIVE

BOXES

The borrowed sneakers struck the sandy road with a sound that was more of a *thuff* than a *thud*. Blue tried to focus on that sound, tried to make it faster.

Thuff, thuff. Think about that. Not the house. Not Ida. Not the relatives or the attic or the boxes or another whole stupid day without a single call from . . .

Blue's chest ached, but he told himself it was just his heart getting stronger, pumping harder. It was sending blood to his feet so that they could get him to the sign in twelve minutes.

Don't think. Just *thuff.*

But Blue had learned that running and thinking went together whether he wanted them to or not, and this morning was no exception.

He couldn't stop worrying. About why his dad hadn't

called. About whether or not he hated Ma Myrtle a little bit for putting them through all of this.

Only a horrible person would feel that way, he was sure. *Ida* wasn't angry with their great-grandmother.

She said that Ma Myrtle *had* just found out she was going to die. She said of course a dying mischief-maker would try to distract herself with a little mayhem. She said it was awfully lucky that Blue had come along when he did to help out.

Blue wished Ida would stop saying things.

He wanted to feel happy about promising to help his cousins win the new fate for Granny Eve, or at least, he wanted to feel noble and selfless. Instead, he felt that old familiar dread. The knowledge that he'd lost before he'd even begun weighed Blue down until it was so heavy he couldn't keep running with it.

He slowed to a jog. Then to a stomp.

Blue stomped down his usual route, glaring at everything around him. Trees, ditches, the little gray house with no curtains that was the only other building on the road. An RV, gleaming red and as huge as a fire engine, was parked outside.

The RV was new. Blue glared at it, too.

Feeling suddenly ridiculous, Blue stopped glaring and took a swipe at the gnats that were swarming around his face. He caught a whiff of his cast and grimaced. He'd been sweating in it on his runs, and it had passed *gross* a while ago.

It was actually a bad dream about Devon breaking his arm that had woken Blue up early that morning. He couldn't go back to sleep, so he'd sat there, staring at the stacks of boxes. Wondering what was in them.

He shouldn't have opened them. He'd thought they'd be stuffed full of holiday ornaments, old photos, and clothes that didn't fit anyone. Wasn't that what people kept in attics?

Not Blue's family.

He'd opened four of them before he'd given up and run away. They were all filled with awards. Blue had found a plaque that said 1st Place District Science Fair. A beauty pageant trophy for Young Miss Brilliant Smile. He'd found medals. Ribbons. Certificates.

There were magazines with Montgomerys on the cover and shiny golden cups with their names engraved on the bases. The boxes, all of them, were filled with words like "Grand Prize" and "Top Place."

Champion. Victor. *Winner.*

In most families, those things would have been kept on a high shelf. Or they would have been tucked away behind glass. But in the Montgomery house they were relegated to the attic with its single dim lightbulb and its bare wooden floor. They had been left up there, abandoned, with the dust and the spiders and Blue.

The attic wasn't a trophy case. It was where you put things you didn't care to think about often.

If Blue had ever won a medal, for anything, he would have kept it somewhere safe. It would have been so special, proof that for at least one shining moment he hadn't come in last.

But maybe, he thought, it was different when you were used to winning.

What if everything was different for someone like that?

A scream lived inside of Blue. He hadn't realized it, but he felt it now. Maybe it had been there since his dad left. Or since that first day when he didn't call. Or maybe . . .

Maybe Blue had been born with it, like his fate, and it had been growing with him all this time. A poisonous vine that had been fertilized too much recently.

Then, from Blue's back pocket, an angry siren sounded. It was his cell phone alarm. The *impossible* twelve-minute timer.

Blue let the scream out.

SIX

TUMBLE

Blue didn't go all the way to the sign that morning. He turned around and trudged back toward his attic instead.

He was watching Howard's sneakers scuff the sand, finally *not* thinking after that scream, when a voice, panting and excited, said, "I'm here to help, and help is here!"

Blue almost leaped out of his shoes.

He had gotten used to being the only one on the road. The other Montgomerys were all too busy fawning over Ma Myrtle to exercise, and besides, he ran early to avoid the worst of the heat.

He spun around and saw that a girl around his own age had appeared behind him.

Her cheeks were flushed as if she'd been out for a run, too, but she was wearing pajama shorts and a nightshirt with a picture of a man in a spangled white jumpsuit on the front.

MAXIMAL STAR, the shirt said in glitter letters. BELIEVE IN BRAVERY!

"Are you having heart trouble?" the girl asked. Her brown eyes were wide. "Abdominal pain?"

"What? No!" said Blue. "Where did you come from?"

The girl's short brown hair stuck up in the back like she hadn't had time to brush it. "Shin splints?" she said. "A stitch in your side?" She waved a white plastic case at him, and Blue realized it was a first aid kit.

"I'm fine."

"I heard you scream."

"No you didn't," said Blue automatically. He felt a blush rising up his neck. "That was somebody else."

The girl squinted. "It was you." Her tone was matter of fact. She stared down at his feet. "Maybe you've got an ingrown toenail."

This girl was weird even by Montgomery standards.

"My toenails are fine," Blue said. "Did you follow me all the way out here?"

Was she spying on him? There was a lot of spying going on at the house. Everyone was sizing up the competition, trying to gather dirt on everybody else so that they could tattle to Ma Myrtle and get a rival disqualified before the next crescent moon rose. In case it was the red one.

It was only seven days away. Blue had spied a new lunar calendar on the wall in the kitchen. The red sickle moon was supposed to appear sometime in the summer—nobody knew exactly when thanks to Ma Myrtle. The relatives seemed to think that the end of May might be summery enough to count.

"You shouldn't waste your time with me," he said to the girl. "I'm Blue."

He assumed she must be a new arrival, since he hadn't seen her around the house before. She probably thought he was some super-powerful Montgomery worthy of espionage.

But the girl only lowered her first aid kit, and said sympathetically, "Everyone feels like that sometimes. Do you want to talk about it?"

It took Blue a minute to get it, even though dumb

jokes about his name had always been the norm at school.

"*No,*" he said. "I'm not *sad.* I'm Blue. Alan's son."

That should do it. His dad wasn't the most famous Montgomery, but he was high on the list. Everyone knew Fast Alan, the racing star.

The girl only blinked. Then she beamed. "Oh! Blue. That's a great name! I call myself Tumble. Are you a Maximal Star fan, too? I've got four copies of *How to Hero Every Day!*"

"No?" Blue said. "Isn't he the guy who has the protein shake infomercials?"

She deflated. "He's so much more than that. I guess you're not a hero in training, then?"

A what? "I'm Blue. You know . . . the one who loses."

"What did you lose?" She looked at the ground as if she expected to find a contact lens he'd dropped.

Blue had thought this Tumble girl would have heard about his curse. It was one of the more memorable ones, after all. "No, I didn't lose a *thing.* I just *lose.*"

Her eyebrows pulled together, and she pursed her lips.

"Like games and sports. That's my curse."

"Your . . . curse?" she said.

"Yes," Blue said impatiently. "That's mine. If you want to be specific, I lose competitions of skill. Ma Myrtle's never going to pick me, so you're wasting your time if you're spying on me because you think I might beat you. I can't beat anyone."

Tumble stood there with her head tilted for so long that Blue was suddenly worried he'd misread the situation.

"What's your fate? I mean . . . do you have a good one or a bad one?"

What if she hadn't been spying on him at all? Or . . . oh no. What if she had one of the really bad fates, so bad that she didn't even want to talk about it? And Blue had just *asked*.

"Hey," he said, "you don't have to tell me. I didn't mean to be a jerk."

She didn't answer.

"And you can stay in my attic if you want!" he added hastily. "I mean, since you just got here and the rooms are all gone. I can sleep in Granny Eve's car or something. It'll be fine."

That snapped her out of it. Tumble shook her head.

"Why would I want to sleep in your attic? I'm from next door."

Blue's brain sputtered as he realized his mistake. The pajamas. Him screaming. Right in front of the gray house.

And he'd just . . .

This girl was . . .

"I mean, I don't like my new room much, so maybe your attic would be better, but I've always got the RV and—"

"You're not a Montgomery."

"I'm Tumble *Wilson*," Tumble said, reaching out for a handshake. "Nice to meet you."

Blue grasped her hand with fingers that felt so clumsy he might as well have been wearing mittens.

"You're normal," he said weakly.

Tumble pistoned his hand up and down. "I prefer," she said, "to think of myself as potentially extraordinary."

SEVEN

HOW TO HERO
EVERY DAY

The Wilson family's RV should have been filled with morning sounds when Tumble made it back home. The coffeepot gurgling in the kitchen area, the tiny shower hissing, and maybe Tumble's dad singing one of his jingles while he washed his hair.

Right now he was writing one for a company that made coconut shampoo. They'd sent so many free samples that the family had been using it to clean everything from their socks to the RV's tires.

Tumble set her first aid kit on the foot of her sofa bed and flopped down on top of her fuzzy blue blanket. Then she closed her eyes and sniffed the air. The RV smelled exactly right. Like a sunscreen factory had exploded all over the place.

But it wasn't right. Not even when Tumble tried to hum the latest version of the jingle to herself.

The Wilsons had arrived at their new house the day before. The trip across the country had been made longer by their infallible GPS failing to recognize Murky Branch's existence.

Who could blame it, though? According to the town sign, three hundred and forty-two people lived here. How was Tumble supposed to be a hero in a place that was almost not a place at all?

Of course, that was exactly what her parents were counting on.

"Uh-oh!" the GPS had said over and over in its determined, friendly voice. "It looks like you've gone off the map!"

Tumble thought that was an omen. Her parents thought it was quaint.

They thought the house was quaint, too. And the town welcome sign. And even their elderly landlord, Mr. Ralph Patty, who had been waiting on their new front porch to hand over the keys. He'd wanted to apologize in person for the fact that the house had no curtains. Apparently, his bonkers dog had destroyed them, along with every last doily and dust ruffle in the place.

When Mr. Patty left (to live with family in Orlando), the Wilsons had spent the whole afternoon unloading the RV and moving in. Tumble had been given her own bedroom for the first time in her life, and her parents had made a big deal about how exciting it was to have so much space to spread out in. They kept pointing out that Tumble's room had a view of the woods, and that she could decorate it herself.

"Posters of Maximal Star everywhere if you want!" her mother had offered.

Considering her mother's feelings about Maximal Star, it was proof that she knew just how thoroughly she had ruined Tumble's life.

But Tumble had smiled. She had nodded. At the end of the day, she had gone to her new room with its new view, and she had even let her parents tuck her in like they had when she was little.

Only she couldn't sleep in the strange house, in the giant room with its thin quilt and its springy, shrieky bed. After growing up in RVs, all of the extra space felt echoing and empty. Her parents, sleeping down the hall, must have been snoring softly as usual, but Tumble couldn't hear them.

Sneaking out to sleep in the RV had seemed like the obvious solution. Her sofa bed was snug, and her fuzzy blanket was soft. But without her parents and their noisy morning routine, it wasn't quite home.

Tumble swallowed down something suspiciously lump-like in her throat. She reminded herself that Maximal Star wouldn't get all weepy over the fact that he had to sleep in a different bed. *Geez, Louise,* she thought in her sternest mental voice. *Get a grip.*

She racked her brain for a quote and found one. *Staying upbeat will vanquish defeat.* That was from the author's note in *How to Hero Every Day.*

Tumble sighed. "Thanks, Maximal," she whispered to the empty RV.

Her parents had taken her life and given it a good hard shake, but that didn't mean Tumble was going to fall to pieces. Heroing was an everyday business after all. And despite all odds Tumble had found someone who needed her on her very first day in Murky Branch.

Blue Montgomery. He was the solution to her problem. After her last rescue had ended . . . dramatically, Tumble's parents had decided she needed stability. Peacefulness. A town so small it would surely bore the heroism right out of her.

They wouldn't be happy to know that they had moved her next door to a strange screaming boy who thought he was honest-to-goodness cursed. Tumble was feeling pretty lucky for the first time in ages.

She took a deep breath, held it, and started to count seconds. This was her current self-improvement exercise, and she made a point of doing it every morning. One day she might see someone drowning, she figured, and if she could hold her breath for two straight minutes, she would absolutely-for-sure be able to save them. Probably.

It might take years, but according to Maximal Star, you had to prepare for these situations well in advance.

Sixty-five, sixty-six, sixty-seven!

Tumble's lungs felt like someone was trying to empty them with a vacuum hose, so she finally gave up and took another breath. Sixty-seven seconds was pretty good. It was two more seconds than yesterday, twenty more seconds than two weeks ago, and over halfway to her goal.

Sixty-seven seconds made her feel confident enough to head into the house. The RV was already getting uncomfortably hot.

The sofa bed creaked when Tumble stood, and it went *poppa-poppa-clang-thwooong* when she folded it up and slammed it into place. Because she hadn't made the bed first, her blanket sprouted from the edges. She thought about taking the blanket with her, into the air-conditioned house, where she would be sleeping that night.

Definitely she would be sleeping there, because she wasn't a baby for goodness' sake.

Of course, she could also wait and come back for the blanket later. If she got cold. She poked it down into the cracks and covered the sofa with its puffy white cushions.

If her dad was where he was supposed to be, in the RV, drying his wet hair with a towel, he would say, "Hey, look at that! Instant living room!"

And Tumble would roll her eyes, because honestly, her dad needed some new jokes.

And her mother would peer blearily at them both and grunt over her cup of coffee.

And . . .

Tumble shook her head at herself. She had found someone to help. That was what mattered.

She crossed the yard, noticing that it was more weeds than grass really, and who was going to take care of that? Her mother knew a lot about engines and suspensions and mechanical stuff, and her dad knew all about coconut shampoo and iambic pentameter. Tumble didn't think either of them knew the first thing about growing a lawn. *That's the kind of problem you should consider before moving into a house.*

And who was going to keep those shiny green bushes at the corner of the house alive? Were they roses? Tumble didn't know what rosebushes looked like if there were no flowers. She hopped up the two steps onto the porch and noticed a hummingbird feeder hanging from the rafters. It was empty. Who was going to figure out what to feed the hummingbirds?

The whole situation was frustrating. Tumble's parents had made this horrible mistake, and she knew it was a little bit her fault for almost dying during her last rescue, but there was nothing else she could have done.

Her archenemy Susan had been shoving that third grader around at the top of the off-limits old bleachers. And Tumble had intervened just in time. And the third grader hadn't broken her silly head open, and it all would have been totally and completely excellent if the bleacher Tumble had chosen to stand on hadn't been rotten.

She pushed away the memory of hanging from the crumbling boards, all of that empty space underneath her.

Heroes take risks, not days off.

The screen door squealed as she opened it.

"I'm still on duty," Tumble said to herself as she stepped inside. "Even when I'm off the map."

EIGHT

TWELVE *X*'S

Mr. Patty's house had swallowed Tumble's whole life, and it still looked emptier than it should have. Their landlord had left the beds and a few pieces of mismatched furniture behind, but there were no decorations, unless you counted hunting-dog-of-the-month wall calendars.

Tumble didn't.

"Lily?" her mother called. "Are you awake?"

Tumble headed into the kitchen. The fluorescent light on the ceiling buzzed and flickered. The floor was green linoleum, dingy with age or grime, and there was only one small window with an empty curtain rod.

Thanks to the curtain-eating dog, Tumble guessed.

Her mother, bent in half over the counter, was unscrewing an outlet cover. Their coffeepot, usually steaming before the sun had risen, stood unplugged beside her.

"Is the outlet broken?" Tumble asked.

"Not for long," her mother said. The plastic cover hit the countertop with a clatter. "Did you like your new room?"

So, they hadn't even noticed she was gone.

It would have been obvious in the RV if they'd woken up and she was out of bed. Tumble guessed that was another thing that was different about living in a house. She wondered why she'd gone to the trouble of leaving a note on her pillow if nobody had bothered to read it.

"Not really. I kind of missed my sofa bed."

"Mr. Patty's mattresses aren't the best." Her mother was shining a flashlight at the outlet now. "We can get you a new one."

"No, no. It'll be fine."

New mattresses were an investment, weren't they? That was like saying they were going to be in the house for long enough to need . . . well, a mattress. Tumble could hold out until her parents came to their senses.

"Are you sure? We don't want you missing out on sleep."

"I'm positive."

Tumble heard the sound of a shower cutting on and then a yelp from the back of the house.

"Oh, hon!" her mother shouted. "The hot and cold water knobs are backward! Sorry!"

After a moment, the familiar sound of Tumble's dad singing the coconut shampoo song drifted into the kitchen.

"Even the water is messed up?" said Tumble. "Isn't that kind of—"

"These are just quirks," her mother interrupted. "Older houses have lots of quirks. That's part of their charm."

Tumble wanted to snort, but she had decided to be mature about all of this.

"Well, quirks are a little inconvenient, aren't they?" she said in her most mature voice. "Like, there weren't a lot of them in the RV, and we've always done just fine with—"

"How about a muffin for breakfast?" Tumble's mother interrupted, sliding off the counter.

"I have to have protein."

Protein built muscle. Muscle was important in case

you passed by the scene of a train accident and had to lift wreckage to free the victims. *If only* . . .

Her mother pursed her lips. "We don't have any eggs."

"That's okay." Tumble had made sure to keep track of the Maximal Star Proper Protein Powder yesterday. Her dad had buried it in a cabinet behind a stack of plates and the hand mixer.

Tumble was onto him.

She beelined for the right cabinet and grabbed the canister. She dumped two heaping scoopfuls of it into the special shaker, which had been buried in a different cupboard behind the very last row of drinking glasses, and turned to the fridge for milk.

"Lily—"

"Call me Tumble, please."

There was a pause, and then a short, sharp sigh. "Fine. Tumble, I really think a muffin, or maybe a yogurt cup—"

"Hey, that's an idea," said Tumble. She wove her arm around an ancient jar of mayonnaise that Mr. Patty had left to grab a strawberry yogurt. "I can add this in, and it'll be like a strawberry milk shake."

Tumble plopped the yogurt into her shaker and slapped the lid closed. She shook it as hard as she could because it might possibly count as an extra arm workout if she put enough effort into it.

"I think I'll go meet the neighbors later today," Tumble said as she shook. "I saw a boy running past this morning."

Her mother looked pleased, as Tumble had known she would. "That's a wonderful idea, sweetheart! Make some new friends. Settle in."

"Right."

"You could wear that dress I bought you last month."

"Mom, *no*," Tumble groaned. "It's all long and floofy."

"I think it would make a good impression."

Tumble didn't wear dresses, or anything that might trip her up in an emergency situation, if she could help it. She especially did not wear dresses that had layers of frothy yellow lace and ruffles hanging down the back.

"It's too hot," said Tumble. "Besides, the neighbor kids might . . . want to play. Outside. And then I'll get all sweaty and nasty in it."

Her mother made disappointed sounds and head-shaking motions and motherly frowns of disapproval, but Tumble managed to slurp down her protein shake and escape from the kitchen without agreeing to wear the awful dress.

She found a better outfit in her new closet. She would wear her second favorite Maximal Star T-shirt, jean shorts, and practical sneakers.

The right equipment for every eventuality. Chapter Two.

Tumble crumpled the note she'd left on the pillow the night before. She didn't have a trash can yet, so she threw it into an empty corner. It bounced off the wall and rolled toward the center of the floor.

It looked out of place there, all by itself.

Tumble flopped back onto the bed, wincing at the shriek and the bounce. Then she dug her hand into her pocket and pulled out a plastic snack bag. It was still securely zipped. Inside the bag was a golf pencil, a picture she'd printed off a library computer in Seattle nearly a year before, and, most importantly, a pink eraser.

She glanced toward the door to make sure it was shut before she took out the picture. Her brother—Jason Wilson. She wondered if she would have called him Jason, or if they would have had special nicknames for each other. Jace and Lils, maybe. Jay. JJ.

She wondered a lot of things like that.

In the photograph, her brother was wearing his football jersey. Two dark stripes were painted under his eyes, and the pads beneath his jersey made him look big as a mountain.

Tumble turned the photo over. Even though she'd taped the edges of the paper, it was getting ragged. Probably from all of the erasing.

The back of the picture had once been covered with *x*'s. Tumble hadn't been too particular about the number. She'd only known that she had to fill the space with them.

Every heroic deed meant she could erase one.

Big things, like saving that third grader on the bleachers, meant she could erase *more* than one. She'd taken off six for that, even though it had gone wrong at the end. Except for stopping that shoplifter in Texas, it was her biggest success so far.

Tumble had twelve *x*'s left. When the back of the

picture was blank, she would feel . . . like she was sup-posed to feel.

Different, she thought. *Better. Braver.*

Maybe she would even feel brave enough to tell her parents she knew the truth. They didn't have to lie to her anymore.

Twelve x's isn't so many. Twelve x's is doable.

But the doing of it might take forever in a place like Murky Branch.

NINE

STARTER
NAMES

By three o'clock that afternoon, Tumble stood at the end of the weed-choked driveway. Her mother was busy working on what seemed to be an issue with the house's plumbing, and Tumble had realized that it was time for her to go if she didn't want to be roped into helping.

Heroism didn't apply to problems with pipes. She was sure of it.

It was hot and sticky humid outside. She looked around to get her bearings, but the closest thing to a signpost was the dented, galvanized mailbox at the end of the drive. 401 R. PATTY was stenciled on the side in black paint.

Tumble opened it. There was nothing inside but pale dust from the road.

The only person who ever sent Tumble mail was her

Grandpa Laffy. He signed a birthday card for her every year. She would be twelve in eight months, and there was no way she'd be here that long.

"You're just going to have to get used to being empty," she told the mailbox.

The ditches were narrow and filled with spiny weeds and briars. They left scratches thin as paper cuts all over Tumble's ankles as she walked until she gave up on proper highway safety and decided to use the middle of the sandy road. Pine trees stood at attention on either side of her. The ground underneath them was covered in a layer of fallen brown needles. And in the shade of the trees, bushes with giant fronds rattled as if creatures were hiding just out of sight.

Palmettos, thought Tumble. That was what her mother had called them. Her mother, who used to visit her grandmother in this place when she was a little girl. Tumble couldn't imagine it.

It wasn't that her mother didn't like nature. She did. But she liked what Tumble thought of as *organized* nature. She liked parks and campgrounds and lakes not too far from cities—the kinds of places where you spent the morning taking pictures of squirrels and then went to the gift shop that afternoon to buy coffee mugs and snow globes.

Tumble was pretty sure there was no such thing as a Murky Branch snow globe.

A few minutes after she had set out, the Montgomery house appeared around the curve. If not for the trees, Tumble would have had a good view of it from her bedroom window.

Mr. Patty had mentioned visitors from out of town, but Tumble hadn't realized just how many cars and trucks would be parked in the yard. She also hadn't pictured something so big. It looked more like a haunted bed-and-breakfast than a home.

Tumble tilted her head and crossed her eyes and decided that the humongous old place wasn't ugly. Just different. And she liked different.

In Chapter Four of *How to Hero Every Day*, Maximal Star talked about how important it was for a hero to differentiate herself from the average person: "People should know from the moment they meet a hero that he is someone special. He is here to help, and help is here."

It was good, Maximal said, to have some way of telling people that you wouldn't stand for evil of any kind. Like, for example, if your name was Maximal Star. That would let people know that you weren't going to sit around if bad things were happening.

Tumble had picked Tumble because it was a good starter name.

She didn't think it would be right for a beginner to choose a name like Maximal; people might get the wrong idea about your abilities. But Tumble was perfect, especially because she had come up with a good Heroic Introduction to go with it.

"I'm Tumble Wilson," Tumble said as she stared at the house. "And I'm ready no matter how rough-and-tumble the situation gets."

Sometimes—a lot of the time—people laughed when Tumble used her introduction. But she liked to think of it as practice. A hero couldn't afford to be embarrassed about doing the right thing, and anyway, the people who laughed the loudest were the ones she knew to watch out for. They'd be the ones knocking younger kids around or writing rude messages on bathroom stalls.

Blue wouldn't be one of those, she thought. He'd be friendly.

She considered walking right up to the front door and asking for him, but he had run off looking so mortified and flustered earlier that she was worried he might refuse to see her.

Anyway, there was an entire chapter devoted to re-connaissance in *How to Hero Every Day*. Tumble would *assess her assets, observe the obstacles, and perceive the path to success.*

When she was finished, Murky Branch wouldn't know what had hit it.

TEN

NORMAL
PEOPLE

B lue finally managed to get his hands on the old-fashioned wall phone in the kitchen when Ma Myrtle summoned the Montgomerys out onto the porch that afternoon. Everyone went except for Blue and his grandmother, who was trying to nap after staying up all night to deal with some late arrivals from Brazil.

Blue's fingers automatically punched in the first few digits of the hotel's number before he remembered. His dad would be on the road by now, following his old racing buddies, talking to people about getting back behind the wheel. That had been his plan the last time Blue had heard it anyway.

He dialed his dad's cell phone instead and waited. It rang over and over until finally the voice mail picked up. "Hello!" said a younger Blue's chipper voice. "You've reached Alan Montgomery. Please leave a message. He'll get back to you almost as fast as he drives."

Blue was getting tired of hearing himself make that joke.

"There you are," Howard said, stepping into the kitchen as Blue hung the phone back on the wall. "Come outside. Ida's terrible at spying and none of them will say anything in front of me or Jenna."

"Your doorknob almost killed me."

"It's low voltage," Howard said without a hint of shame. "Anyway, spying's not so bad. Greg's made sandwiches."

"Who?"

"The guy from California who starts fires?" Howard shrugged. "Apparently he's big on cold cuts, and he's decided that the way to a brand-new fate is through Ma Myrtle's stomach."

"I can't believe *you're* leaving food behind."

"I'm noble like that. Sacrificing myself for the greater good and all."

Blue thought about it. "You got into another argument with Ma Myrtle, didn't you?"

Howard opened the fridge then slammed the door when he saw it was empty. "No. But I was about to."

He ran a hand through his bangs. "She started in on the whole 'upholding the family honor by eating everything in sight' thing again. I thought it would be better to leave."

Because he didn't want to ruin their chances, Blue knew. Because he didn't want to mess it up for Granny Eve.

"I can't believe she's doing this," Blue said. "Granny Eve is her daughter."

Howard leaned back against the counter. "I can't believe Granny Eve hasn't put a stop to it," he replied. "Or at least kicked all of these buzzards out and told them to find motels. She would have *usually*. But I think this death-date business has thrown her into a tailspin." He made a vague twirling gesture with one hand.

"She seems okay," Blue said. "Mostly."

"Yeah, but she's Granny Eve." Howard frowned at a fridge magnet from Flat's Restaurant. "She's supposed to be more than okay."

Blue ate half of a cucumber cream-cheese sandwich and tried to listen to three conversations at once.

Some of the relatives had crammed themselves around Ma Myrtle's spot on the porch swing. The others were left to stew around the edges and plot.

As soon as people realized who Blue was, he turned invisible. "That's the loser boy," they whispered. "Don't worry about him."

One of the Brazilian cousins had helped him get to the sandwich tray, and Ernestine, the college girl with electrical problems, had waved at him before she went back to strumming a ukulele at Ma Myrtle's feet. Blue added those two to his very short mental list of Montgomerys who weren't terrible and decided not to eavesdrop on them.

Instead, he focused on the singing toddler's mother, the car accident lady, and a foul-smelling uncle who was painting Ma Myrtle's portrait.

The toddler was standing next to Ma Myrtle, singing a twangy song about duck hunting. He was all chubby cheeks and smiles, and he was doing a little dance that involved tapping the heels of his cowboy boots against the porch boards and spinning. His name was Chet, and everyone agreed he was a threat.

"I didn't expect it to be a little kid who ruined it all," the car accident woman was grumbling. Her leg was trapped in a medical boot, and she had stitches running across her forehead. "If Ma Myrtle says *darling* or *angelic* one more time, I'm going to swat Chelsea with my crutches."

Chelsea was the toddler's mother. Blue didn't know what her fate was, so it couldn't have been spectacularly good or bad. But she was spectacularly annoying. She was sure that, any day now, Ma Myrtle would be telling her how to find the alligator under the red moon.

"It's all for Chet's sake you know," she was saying to a cousin with a handlebar mustache. "He's the youngest one here, so he has the most to gain from a new fate. It only makes sense!"

"And the rest of us can just get lost and die miserable, is that it?" Mustache snorted. "Your kid already *has* a great life ahead of him with that talent. Why don't you just keep riding his coattails all the way back to Nashville and let the rest of us have a chance?"

"Exactly what I was thinking!" said a thin woman with an accent Blue didn't recognize.

Cousin Chelsea sniffed and tried to flip her poofy hair over her shoulder disdainfully, but she'd applied so much hairspray that her hairdo only crunched at the impact.

"Excuse me!" she said. She flounced off and started shoving and jostling her way through the crowd around Ma Myrtle.

"Good riddance," said Mustache.

"She's a harpy," the stinky painter muttered. He had moved his easel to the porch steps. The stench was his curse; painting was just a hobby he was hoping would be enough to win Ma Myrtle over. Like the fire starter with his trays of sandwiches and Ernestine with her ukulele.

Blue had eaten the last bite of cucumber cream cheese, but he didn't feel like fighting his way across the porch to get another one. Besides, listening to the bitter words and angry mutters all around him had ruined his appetite.

I won't be like these people, he promised himself. *No matter what, I won't.*

He stepped over to the edge of the porch, trying to ignore the chaos for a few seconds. It was a hot, bright day, and Granny Eve's yard blazed with different shades of green. The grass was long, except for the trails made by the relatives' cars and trucks driving through it. Someone was drying their laundry on the side of the chicken coop.

Motion caught Blue's eye and he glanced above the coop. One of the pecan tree's limbs was shaking. He squinted through the leaves and saw a flash of yellow fabric.

Someone was up there. In the tree. Spying on the Montgomerys, just like Blue was.

Blue scanned all the people on the porch, wondering who was missing. He didn't know every single face in the house, but a quick head count gave him the right number. So it was someone who'd just gotten here. Or . . .

A new suspicion gnawed at Blue. He stared as hard as he could up into the tree, but all he saw was that scrap of yellow and the edge of a shoe.

Smart people, thought Blue, *stay away when you tell them you're cursed. Normal people think you've lost your marbles.*

The alligator carved onto the column nearest him seemed to be smiling through its crooked teeth.

Normal doesn't belong, it reminded Blue. *Not in this place.*

ELEVEN

FRIENDS IN HIGH PLACES

Tumble's hand was starting to cramp from bracing herself against the limb near her head, and her ankles ached from balancing for so long. But giving into discomfort wasn't an option. Maximal Star had once crawled through a tunnel for three miles with broken ribs to save a trapped miner.

Climbing the big tree would have been impossible, but Tumble had *assessed her assets* and used the hutch in the empty chicken coop to get aloft. And it was worth it. More than that!

She'd been hoping to get information that would help her help Blue, but what she'd gotten was even better. Here was a whole family who needed a hero! Blue's delusions were genetic. The Montgomerys, at least most of them, thought they were honest to goodness cursed.

It had taken Tumble a while to be sure that they were

all one family, but after listening for over an hour, she was certain of that much. They didn't look alike, and at least one of them spoke mostly Portuguese, but they all addressed each other as Cousin or Aunt or Great-Great-Uncle.

Tumble had soon realized that the center of everything was a tiny, ancient woman named Ma Myrtle. She was sitting on the porch swing, wearing a sundress and a straw hat with a wide brim perched on top of her long white hair. She was plucking finger sandwiches from a plastic tray that a scrawny, bearded guy was holding out to her.

As Tumble listened in on the noisier members of the family, a picture of what was going on started to build itself in her head. Some ancestor of theirs had found *something* a long time ago in the swamp that had made him rich enough to build this monster of a house. But they thought he'd also cursed them in the process. And there was a lot of talk about the moon and the occasional mention, in high nervous tones, of a golden alligator.

Tumble had worked hard to piece this all together into a story that made sense. She had finally decided that the legend must be about an ancient Montgomery finding a cursed alligator statue in the Okefenokee, then melting it down for the money.

Not bad, as far as adventure stories went. Tumble would have added a few explosions and a swamp witch if she were making it up. But maybe the original maker-upper had thought that would be too much.

Pleased that she had figured the puzzle out, Tumble turned her attention back to the porch to see that a woman with poofy hair was misting Ma Myrtle with a squirt bottle full of ice water to keep her cool.

When the little singing boy stopped, the old woman applauded and every eye turned toward her. "Wonderful!" she said. Tumble could only make out every other word or so when Ma Myrtle spoke. "I do have . . . and an ear . . . musical arts."

The poofy-haired lady looked like she might burst from excitement. She lifted her squirt bottle higher and started spritzing wildly.

"My Chet is such a talent!" she said loudly enough for everyone, including Tumble, to hear. *Spritz, spritz.* "Everyone in Nashville says it!" *Spritz, spritz, spritz.*

Wait a second. *Where did he go?*

Blue had vanished while Tumble was figuring out the whole thing. Oh no. An experienced hero never took her eyes off the person she was trying to help.

She leaned forward, trying to get a good angle to see the entire porch.

"It's rude to eavesdrop on people."

Startled to hear the voice coming from *over* her head, Tumble whirled. She wobbled and lost her balance. She had just a second to see Blue Montgomery lying across the limb above her, his broken arm dangling and his blond hair full of leaves, then her shoes slipped.

Blue's arm shot out toward Tumble, and her scrabbling fingers grasped his cast just in time.

He yelped. The arm was *almost* healed, but it still hurt to have a girl hanging off it.

"Sorry," he gasped, holding tightly on to his limb to brace against her weight. "I'm sorry! I didn't mean to scare you."

Not true. He had absolutely meant to scare her, but only a *little* bit. Only enough to make her go away and make himself feel better about the fact that she'd over-heard his freak-out that morning.

Tumble clutched his cast with both hands as she maneuvered herself back toward the tree's trunk. She was breathing hard.

"Just like the bleachers," she panted. "So far down."

Her face had gone white, and her eyes were popping. Since Blue had last seen her, her short hair had been brushed and pulled back into a tiny sprout of a ponytail.

"Are you okay?" Blue asked when she didn't let go of his cast.

"Ha!" said Tumble. She swallowed. "I'm fine. I almost fell off something a few weeks back, too. Some bleachers at my old school. What are the chances, right?"

Great. Blue had thought it was pretty sneaky and smart to climb up the tree without her noticing. Now he felt guilty.

"I'm sorry."

"It's not your fault," Tumble said, finally dropping his arm. "Just me being clumsy."

And now he felt worse. "You *were* spying on us."

Tumble nodded. "Only because I wanted to get to know you better."

Blue frowned. "Why?"

"So we can be friends of course! We got off to a weird start this morning, but I just moved here. And from what I overheard, it sounds like you just moved here, too? So . . ."

Excitement at the idea of befriending him seemed to have put her nerves out of her mind. She was even bouncing a little on the balls of her feet, making the limb underneath her tremble.

Reminding Blue that he *had* almost scared her out of a tree. "Uh . . . okay." He wondered how bad this idea was. "But you should know that the situation is kind of unusual around here."

Tumble grinned at him as if to say she ate unusual for breakfast.

I loathe interruptions to the natural order of things, but I think I will indulge myself. We'll meet after all, you and I, and I don't care to endure your mistaken impressions.

I am no statue.

I am not a prize to be won.

And despite Tumble Wilson's wild imaginings, I do not melt.

Hello, I suppose. You can't have my name. It's not for your kind.

You can call me what the Montgomerys do.

Call me Munch.

TWELVE

A HEROIC PLAN OF ACTION

Ever since she'd gotten serious about heroism, trouble had a strange effect on Tumble. On the one hand, she didn't *want* anyone to be in dire straits, but on the other, dire straits meant that she could do something to help. And that sent a giddy, guilty jolt of energy through her.

The Montgomerys were the best of both worlds. They weren't actually in danger, but most of them *thought* they were. Blue had explained a few things. Fate and weird moons and magic alligators—Tumble had never heard anything like it outside of fairy tales.

All the Montgomerys needed was someone to show them they were being superstitious and silly. Tumble could help them without doing anything risky. Even her parents couldn't object.

Not that she gave them the opportunity to try. She

led them to believe that the neighbors were absolutely ordinary, and that her new friend was the ordinariest of them all.

"Blue's really nice," she told her mother the next morning over breakfast. "He's got a broken arm, though, so I'm going to take some board games with me to cheer him up."

Her mother hesitated, coffee mug hovering in front of her lips. "Is *Blue* a Maximal Star fan, too?"

"No," said Tumble. "But give me time."

They found Eve Montgomery's number in an old phone book in the living room, and her mother called to be sure that Tumble was invited. Tumble leaned over the back of the sofa, crossing her fingers and hoping that none of the weirder Montgomerys picked up.

"What a pleasant lady," Tumble's mother said, plunking the phone back into its cradle. "Blue's grandmother says you should feel free to come over any time. Mrs. Eve is going to send you home with some zucchini from her garden."

So Blue *did* have some normal relatives. Tumble would have to incorporate them into her heroic action plan. She might need allies to convince the more stubborn members of the family to see reason.

But first—Blue.

She was so excited she would have skipped the whole way over if her arms weren't loaded with board games. After questioning a few people, she found Eve Montgomery in the kitchen. She was thick around the middle, with curly gray hair, and when Tumble met her, she was staring into a refrigerator that was bare of everything but a jar of pickle juice.

"I'm here to see Blue," said Tumble. "My mom called."

"You two are friends?" Eve asked, shutting the fridge.

"Yes," said Tumble. "I brought games."

She gestured with the boxes in her arms. Parcheesi almost slipped off the top, and Eve reached over to shove it back in place.

"Well, I'm not sure he'll take to *that* idea," she said. "But I'm glad he's got a friend. He's been a little down. Wasn't expecting to spend his summer here, and his daddy . . . well . . . if the games don't work out, you can always come and help me in the garden."

She gave Tumble directions to the attic and promised

to send up lunch if she could find any food.

Tumble wended her way through the house to a narrow door at the top of the third floor landing. It opened onto a steep, musty-smelling staircase. Tumble paused to review her plan.

She figured as long as she spoke reasonably and didn't laugh at Blue for his superstitions, she'd be marking off another *x* that afternoon.

All right. I've got this.

"Hello!" she called. "It's Tumble Wilson! I've had an idea about your problem." She adjusted her grip on the games and teetered up the stairs.

When Blue finally said, "Come in," she had almost reached the top.

The last step into the attic was the steepest, and Tumble stumbled her way up it. The floorboards were bare wood, and the rafters sloped so that you couldn't stand straight up at the edges of the room. It was a large but gloomy space. The only spots of brightness were a pull-chain bulb overhead and a poster covered in paint splotches that had been taped to a tower of plastic storage containers.

A half-circle window set in the wall opposite Tumble would have let in light, but it was mostly covered by boxes. She thought the view might be good from so high up if someone moved all of the junk out of the way.

Blue was sitting on top of an air mattress in the middle of the floor, staring at his cell phone. A lumpy duffel bag was behind him, its zipper gaping open to reveal piles of rumpled clothes.

"Is it the cell service?" Tumble asked. "We don't get it at our house, either. We *barely* get Internet."

It had taken her an hour to log on to Maximal Star's website and update her fan club profile with the new house's address.

"Yeah," said Blue. "It's like that here. I was just checking."

He dropped the phone back into his duffel and waved an arm around at the attic. "Welcome to my room."

"It's . . . interesting."

Blue sighed. "The house is really crowded."

"I'll bring you a blanket or something the next time I come," Tumble promised, eyeing the air mattress. "I've been thinking about your issue."

"My issue?"

"Right," she said, setting the games down on the floor. "Your losing issue."

"It's not an issue," he said bluntly. "It's a curse."

"Can I sit down?"

He shrugged, and she stepped over to his mattress. She plopped down beside him.

"Curses," she said, hoping Blue wouldn't notice that she'd rehearsed. "Sometimes everyone feels like they're cursed. I've felt that way myself lately."

She bounced a couple of times on the mattress. "I mean, I got expelled from my last school for saving a kid's life. How unfair is that? And a few months ago I was in this convenience store, and I saw this man slipping a bottle of organic lemonade into his jacket—"

"It's not the same."

Tumble decided to ignore the interruption. "The thing about your particular problem," she said, "is that it's very easy to test."

"What?"

"I'm going to prove that you're not a loser. You can win anything if you want."

"How are you going to prove something like that?"

Tumble stood. "I'm glad you asked!"

She sprang over to the board games and started holding them up one by one. "These are some of my favorites," she said. "I've got Scrabble! Monopoly! Tiddlywinks!"

"Okay?" said Blue.

"Seriously," said Tumble. "If we play enough games, I swear, you will *eventually* win one. Nobody loses every time. Nobody."

She was going to make Blue believe her. It wasn't just that she didn't think alligators hid in the swamp waiting to jinx people. It was that the idea of a world where a person could literally be cursed, no matter what he did or how hard he tried, offended every last bit of her.

Not everything was fair. Tumble knew that better than most people. But the world had to be fairer than *that*.

"Listen," said Blue, "this is really nice of you, but you don't—"

"Oh, *come on* . . ." Tumble pleaded. "We've got all day. And if you don't win a game *then* I'll know you're right. And I'll help you uncurse yourself! This time you've got nothing to lose."

"*Uncurse* myself?" Blue asked.

"Well, if curses were real—which they're not!—but if curses were real they could obviously be broken. It's in all the books and movies, right? If you don't win something today, I'll just figure out how to uncurse you. That's a much better idea than trying to make Ma Myrtle pick you over all of the others before this moon deadline thing comes up."

Tumble was proud of this argument. It was her backup-backup plan. If Blue believed in cursedness, he had to believe in uncursedness, too. So if all else failed, Tumble would still have a way to move forward.

"I don't . . . I'm not trying to . . ." Blue frowned. "I'm not like the rest of them, okay? I'm actually trying to help Howard, Jenna, and Ida save Granny Eve from her fate."

"What's her fate?"

Blue went quiet.

Tumble wondered if that was considered a rude question in his family.

"Her husbands die," he said finally.

Tumble felt her eyebrows trying to climb her forehead. She forced them to stay in place.

"I'm only telling you so that you won't mention it to her. Let's just play some games and when I lose—"

"When you win," Tumble said firmly, "you'll agree to read *How to Hero Every Day*. I put a copy in with the Monopoly board. Deal?"

Blue shrugged.

Tumble pulled Scrabble out of the stack and settled cross-legged onto the floor in front of him. She set up the board and then held the bag full of tiles out to Blue. He looked at it like it might hold live tarantulas.

Tumble gave the bag a little shake. "Come on," she said. "If you don't like Scrabble, we can try something else next. We can even race if you want. You like to run, right? And I think I saw a dartboard in one of Mr. Patty's closets."

"No!" said Blue, his hand diving into the bag of tiles. "Scrabble's great. The best. Just . . . no darts."

"Why not?"

He stared down at the letters in his hand. "You'll see."

THIRTEEN

A WINK
AND A NOD

"Scrabble was fine!" Tumble tried to explain to Blue's frantic, rainbow-haired cousin Ida. Eve Montgomery was loading Blue into her Thunderbird for a trip to the emergency room. Tumble couldn't believe things had gone so wrong.

"Scrabble!" shouted Ida, like it was a kind of deadly weapon.

The two of them were arguing in the front yard instead of helping Jenna move the twins' car like they were supposed to. The Civic had been penned in between a van and a motorcycle, and Jenna was trying to maneuver it out of the way so that Eve's Thunderbird could escape from its own tight spot.

"Yes, Scrabble!" said Tumble. "Scrabble was totally boring."

She waved Jenna to the left just in time to keep her from running into the motorcycle.

"Boring doesn't mean safe! He could have lost an eye!"

Ida was waving, too. The wrong way. Jenna honked the horn at them.

Tumble had had a good plan for Scrabble. But Blue was sharper than she had anticipated. "You can't lose on purpose," he'd told her when she tried to misspell *query*. "It doesn't count if you lose on purpose."

So they had switched to Monopoly. Tumble was unfortunately great at Monopoly.

Finally, when they settled on tiddlywinks, it started working. Tumble was good, but even playing with his left hand, Blue was some kind of tiddlywinks prodigy. She was losing, and as the game went on, she could tell Blue was getting more and more hopeful.

He'd laughed and joked around and told her more about his family and how their lives were all controlled by great and terrible fates. He admitted that he'd lost a fight with a boy at school and that was part of the reason why his dad had left him in Murky Branch.

"It's not fair," he'd said, "because he was the one who told me I had to stand up for myself, and then when I do, he gets mad. Or upset. Or something. And leaves me here."

He had glared at a green wink. "And I'm the one who should be mad. I mean, I have the broken arm."

"So what's your dad's fate?" Tumble had asked in order to change the subject.

"The opposite of mine. He wins. Not like the lottery or coin tosses, but anything that takes skill. He was a race car driver. He won all the time . . . unless he threw the race on purpose. He had to do that every now and then to deflect suspicion, you know?"

Tumble knew it sounded fishy. How could Blue be sure his dad had lost those races on purpose? Maybe it was all a ploy. And if he was such a hotshot racer, why had he quit?

But when she asked, Blue said, "Maybe because of the wrecks. There were some bad ones right before he quit. He wasn't involved in any of them, but it must have soured things a little." He shrugged. "His last girlfriend said it was just because he's such a free spirit."

Tumble bit her tongue. She had tried to point out inconsistencies with the other family members' alleged curses, only to have Blue neatly poke holes in each theory. He had an explanation for *everything*.

Until he started to win at tiddlywinks.

He was popping the plastic winks into the cup. *Plock, plock, plock.* And he was getting more and more excited, and so was Tumble because she was going to be the one who saved Blue from his imaginary fate, and then . . .

Blue's grandmother said he would be fine.

"Nobody ever went blind from getting hit in the eye with a tiddlywink," she said when Tumble dashed downstairs to get help. "Not even in this house."

Jenna honked the horn again, and Tumble's brain snapped back to the present. She hurried out of the way.

"Are you sure you don't want me to come with you?" Ida called as Eve finally pulled the Thunderbird forward.

"We'll be fine," Eve said through her open window. "Just keep an eye on this bunch until I get back. Especially Ma Myrtle."

Ida nodded.

Tumble waved as the Thunderbird passed. Blue waved

back. He was squinting at her through his uninjured eye, his face thoughtful.

"You *almost* won!" she shouted.

And he nodded.

Tumble's heart lifted. She was betting a lot on that nod. She was betting that he would keep trying, at least, even if she did have to change tactics a little. *What better way to uncurse yourself than to win something?* she would say.

She waved until Eve Montgomery's car was out of sight, then she turned her steps toward home. It was time for a different kind of competition, one that Blue couldn't—not in a million years—lose.

FOURTEEN

A TARNISHED CENT

The ER nurse said Blue's eyeball would heal. It had only been scratched by an unidentified flying object. Granny Eve had very kindly not told the nurse that the UFO in question was a tiddlywink.

They left the hospital with a bottle of eyedrops and instructions to come back later in the week to see about removing Blue's cast.

On the way home, he took advantage of the long car ride and the distance from Murky Branch to call his dad from his cell phone. It took three tries, but he finally picked up.

"Hey there, Skeeter. How are things?" He sounded like himself. Easygoing, relaxed.

"Dad!" said Blue, surprised despite himself. "Hi! I'm in the car with Granny Eve right now, so we can talk."

"Tell him I said hello," Granny Eve said.

"Granny Eve says hello," Blue repeated. "How are you? Did you get my messages about how many relatives have moved in? I'm sleeping in the attic now."

Blue hadn't, necessarily, expected his dad to react to this news with shock and horror. He had never been an overly protective parent. He'd taught Blue to swim by tying parachute cord around his waist and then dangling him in the deep end of a hotel pool until he started to paddle. But Blue had thought he might get a *little* sympathy.

"That's good," his dad said. "Gives you a chance to get away from them all. And you'll have a space to yourself."

This struck Blue as a strange take on the situation. Blue had *always* had a space to himself. He'd always had his own room when they lived in apartments, and he'd had his own room when they lived in hotels.

"Well . . . it's kind of dirty up there."

"I'm sure your granny can help you fix it up nice."

It was true that Granny Eve was trying. She'd stopped by a store on the way back from the hospital and bought Blue a lamp and a new pillow and a set of sheets. But that wasn't the point. The point was that Blue was living in an *attic*. And not even a clean one.

"Where are you staying?" Blue asked. At a hotel, he knew. A fancy one.

"I'll send your granny some money to buy stuff for you. Ask her how much she needs."

"I don't want her to have to buy stuff for me," said Blue. "I want you to come get me early."

His dad didn't answer. Then, in a gruff voice, he said, "We talked about this. I'm making some decisions right now, and it's best if you're with your granny. And with Ma Myrtle dying . . . you should spend time with your great-grandma, too."

Blue's insides clenched. They hadn't known Ma Myrtle was dying when his dad left. And if his dad knew now . . . that meant he *had* been getting Blue's messages.

"Dad—"

"Ask your granny how much money she needs."

Blue didn't want to do that. But then he thought about the sheets and the lamp and the fact that his grandmother was putting up with a whole houseful of people who weren't helping her with the bills.

"Granny Eve?" he said stiffly. "He wants to know how much money you need. To watch me. Just until the end of summer."

Granny Eve raised her eyebrows. Blue saw her grip on the steering wheel tighten. "Not a tarnished cent," she said. "I've got more than enough to take care of you."

Maybe that was true, but Blue had begun to understand that his grandmother didn't tell people when she needed help. She was always the one who did the helping, whether that meant holding her tongue while Ma Myrtle had fun ordering the relatives around or taking in a grandson she hadn't seen in years.

"She says a few hundred dollars should cover it," Blue told his dad.

Granny Eve shot him a look.

"Good," his dad said. "I'll have it to her soon."

He sounded relieved.

"We're getting close to Murky Branch," said Blue. "I guess the phone will die."

"Okay. Take care."

"Remember to check your messages," said Blue. Maybe

he'd heard about Ma Myrtle from someone else. "I've left you a few."

His dad didn't answer. The call had dropped.

Granny Eve shook her head. "I wish you hadn't done that. I really don't need your daddy's money."

"It's fair," said Blue. "He didn't even tell you he was going to bring me here. And with all the other relatives eating everything in the house—"

"That's not for you to worry about," she said.

"He didn't mind anyway," Blue grumbled. "He said he'd send it."

Granny Eve turned the Thunderbird off the highway. Clouds of dust chased them down the dirt road.

"Sometimes," she said in a measured voice, "people would rather give you money than other, harder things."

"Like what?"

"Like their time. Don't go asking for money when what you want is something more valuable, Blue."

FIFTEEN

RECKLESS

The next morning, Howard and the twins woke Blue up early with buckets, mops, and brooms in their hands.

"Granny Eve insisted we help you clean." Jenna yawned as she dragged a stack of boxes to the edge of the room. "I don't know why it couldn't have waited until after lunch."

It wasn't a terrible job, especially not with company, and after half an hour Granny Eve brought up two plates filled with biscuits and fig preserves. "One plate for Howard," she said. "One for the rest of you. And I hope you enjoy it because it's the last of the groceries until someone picks up more."

With food in hand, even Jenna stopped complaining, and Howard was having a wonderful time making fun of Blue.

"It was a wink!" he said, sprawling across Blue's air mattress and shoving a biscuit into his mouth. He swallowed. "You almost got blinded by a tiddlywink. I want to make so many jokes."

"I don't!" Ida exclaimed. She was trying to rearrange the boxes full of trophies around the window so that Blue would be able to see out. "Blue, what were you thinking? People like us have to be careful! Do you see me with gerbil treats glued to my forehead? No! Because I don't want to encourage Jenna's pets to chew my face off."

"The Gerbellion wouldn't do that," said Jenna. "They know you're off-limits."

"I was thinking that I've had enough of losing," said Blue. "I was thinking that trying a few board games was better than trying nothing at all."

He looked around, wondering what to do with his new beanbag chair. Howard had carried it up the stairs, but Blue had a feeling it was another gift from Ida. It was hot pink with yellow polka dots. Not exactly Howard's style. And from what little Blue had seen of her, Jenna enjoyed exciting colors like white and beige.

"It's a good thing you didn't let the neighbor girl talk

you into something really dangerous," said Howard, still snorting with laughter. "Like Go Fish."

"Howard!"

"It's fine, Ida." Blue hauled a box labeled A. MONT-GOMERY out of the way to make room for the beanbag. It was a box he'd been careful not to open. The A could have stood for a lot of Montgomerys, but Blue thought the handwriting looked familiar. He didn't need to see any more trophies, especially ones with his dad's name on them.

"Howard's right. It's stupid for a game of tiddlywinks to be dangerous. And it's ridiculous to be scared all the time of people picking fights with me."

"Hey," said Howard, worry creasing his forehead. "I didn't mean it like that. I was just kidding ar—"

"And I hate it," Blue said. "I *hate* that the whole family ignores me because I'm too much of a loser to matter."

Ida gasped. "Blue! You matt—"

"So I'm not going to do it anymore." Blue liked that he sounded calm. Steady. Like the kind of person who made important decisions and stuck with them. "Tumble Wilson's going to help me break my curse."

The attic fell silent. When Blue looked up, he saw that even Jenna was eyeing him with a worried expression on her face.

"*Whoa,*" said Howard. "Back up. That's not a good idea."

"It's the only idea that makes sense."

"No," said Ida, shaking her head wildly. "No, it's a *horrible* idea."

"You're not going to do anything rash, are you?" Jenna asked. "Because I'm pretty sure Montgomerys have tried to break their fates before. And I'm pretty sure we would know if it had worked."

Blue stared back down at the box. At that spiky letter *A*.

"Blue," said Howard, in the most serious tone Blue had ever heard him use, "we all know about having parents who are cra—"

"Complicated!" shouted Ida.

Howard rolled his eyes. "Yeah. Complicated. But you don't want to make things even more *complicated* by getting reckless."

Blue rounded on them. "Reckless isn't bad when you've

got nothing to lose. Maybe if other Montgomerys had been more reckless we wouldn't be in this mess."

Ida looked faint. "What are you going to do?"

"I'm not going to be a doormat ever again. Not even for fate."

SIXTEEN

THE RACE

"On three?" said Tumble.

It was midmorning, and she and Blue were standing together on the dirt road, ready to race. Tumble had promised to give her one hundred percent best effort, but they had agreed she could take some measures to make running more difficult. She was wearing a down-stuffed parka, the frothy yellow dress her mother liked, and a pair of tall, camouflage boots they had found in the twins' room.

"Snake boots," Blue had explained. "So snakes can't get Ida's legs."

Tumble made a mental note to fix Ida's problem as soon as possible. If she wore these things on her feet every day, the poor girl had suffered enough.

The race would be from mailbox to mailbox. To be

safe, they'd walked all the way to Tumble's driveway and back, scanning the road for things that might trip Blue while he was running. He had even glued the knots on his shoelaces so that they couldn't come undone. As long as he was careful, as long as a meteor didn't fall from the sky on top of him, he would win.

And Tumble would be one *x* closer to her own goal.

The thought lit her up like someone had given her a fresh set of batteries. "All right," she said. "Let's do this."

"One," said Blue.

"Two," said Tumble

"Three!" they shouted together.

Tumble took off, running hard. She'd promised not to hold back, and she didn't. Even in the boots she was setting a quick pace.

But Blue passed her before they were a third of the way to the Wilson's mailbox.

Go, Blue. Go!

She didn't have enough breath to cheer out loud, but in her head, Tumble was waving pom-poms.

■ ■ ■

Blue heard the snake boots hitting the packed sand behind him, out of sync with his own swifter steps. Tumble
wasn't giving up.

But the road ahead of him was clear.

There was a soaring feeling in his chest that didn't
have anything to do with how fast he was running.

What if . . . ? he thought.

What would it be like to reach the mailbox?

What would it be like to make that phone call to his
dad? The one where he said, "You were wrong. Everything can be different if I just try hard enough. I don't
need to find the alligator. You don't need to be embarrassed. I can win. I can."

I can, I can, he thought with every step. He ran faster.
He could see the silver-gray mailbox.

Tumble had to be far behind him now, and every step
he took was one step closer to victory.

Tumble's legs burned from the weight of the boots. Her
dress dug into her armpits, and underneath her heavy
coat, she was dripping like a faucet.

But she was happy, because Blue looked like he had wings.

His whole life would be better once he knew that he was wrong about being a loser, and Tumble would have done something really *good*. No mishaps. No mistakes. Just her being the hero she'd been training and trying to be for so long.

Then came the deer.

It leaped from the woods, a graceful blur as it soared over the ditch. Tumble didn't even have time to shout "Look out!" before it smashed into Blue.

The deer rolled. Blue rolled. Dust flew.

Tumble stumbled to a halt.

The deer was staggering upright. It was big. A beautiful orange-red color, with such wide black eyes. So innocent looking.

Without even glancing at Tumble, the doe shook herself off and darted into the woods on the other side of the road.

Blue stared at the bloody gash on his shin.

"Yikes!" Tumble hunkered over him. Her eyes were

wide. "Does this kind of thing happen a lot around here? Deer just tackling people for no good reason?"

"I don't think so." Blue pressed at the gaping edges of his wound. He winced. "I think I'm just lucky."

"Don't *do* that," said Tumble. She threw off her coat and crouched lower. "Your fingers have germs. You probably need stitches."

Gnats were trying to settle on Blue's leg. Tumble waved them away.

"The clever hero is never underprepared," she muttered. "I forgot my first aid kit, but it's not far to the RV. I've got butterfly tape and antiseptic."

Blue bit his lip and stared at the rivulets of red pouring down the sides of his shin to stain his sock. He hated to admit it, but Tumble was probably right about the stitches. The gash stung and throbbed, and it didn't look like it was going to stop bleeding any time soon.

"I was *so* close," he said, looking toward the mailbox.

"You were," said Tumble. "Three-quarters of the way at least. See? You're not a loser."

"If it wasn't the deer, it would have been something else."

"I don't believe that," Tumble said in that *way* she had. As if she could make the world behave itself just because she said so. "Blue, you can win. You were about to. The finish line is there."

Blue gazed at the entrance to the Wilsons' driveway. So close. Just yards away really. "I want to finish the race."

"You do?"

He nodded. He could feel it, the almost-victory. What if the trick was to keep trying? What if he had kept on playing tiddlywinks with one good eye?

He wanted to know, once and for all, just how badly it could go wrong.

"You . . . probably do need stitches, though," said Tumble. She looked torn. Blue guessed Maximal Star didn't recommend letting wounded victims run off into further danger.

"If you can race in that outfit, then I can race with a little cut on my leg."

Tumble squinted at the mailbox. "I guess it's not that far."

Blue was already climbing to his feet.

"Okay," said Tumble, nodding. "Yeah. That's the spirit. 'Falling down doesn't mean you've fallen for good!'"

Blue wondered if she had an endless supply of those quotes stuffed into her brain. He wondered if Maximal Star had ever saved someone from fate itself.

SEVENTEEN

BEAST

Tumble was glad she'd left the parka off this time. Her feet were drowning in sweaty pools as it was, and she was sure she was going to have blisters.

Blue took the lead right away, sticking to the precise center of the road so that he would have time to see any oncoming wildlife. Tumble swung her legs and arms as hard as she could, but she was never going to catch up. *It's going right this time*, she thought. *He's going to do it for sure. That's two x's at least.*

Her lungs ached.

Maybe three.

"No! No! Stop! Heel!" It was a man's voice somewhere behind her. Shouting.

Tumble heard a powerful bark. She slowed to look over her shoulder. And saw . . . it was . . . behind her, there was a monster.

A dog. Gigantic. A brindle brute made of hungry teeth. And it was flinging itself toward Tumble like she'd rung its dinner bell.

Someone was chasing the dog, but Tumble didn't wait to figure out who. She shrieked in a very unheroic way and fled. She felt, more than saw, the dog leaping for her backside.

Suddenly, the heavy snake boots were the fastest shoes she'd ever worn. She heard a shredding sound and felt a yank at the back of her dress.

It's biting me! she thought. *Bitingmebiting! Teethteethteeth!*

Tumble's whole body turned into a single screaming need to *RUN*.

Blue heard someone shouting behind him, and then Tumble was screeching, and then, before he could figure out what was going on, Tumble was passing him.

She was a human comet, a blur of trailing yellow ruffles. And a huge dog with brown-streaked fur was snapping at her like it wanted to gnaw her knees off.

Blue's pounding heart skipped a beat. Then he took off after the dog.

"Run, run, run!" he cried.

Tumble ran right past her own driveway and kept going.

A moment later, Blue saw her stagger. He tried to push himself faster, but he was already running as fast as he could.

Tumble fell. The dog dove.

She was yelling.

Blue was yelling.

Someone far behind them was yelling.

And the dog was diving again and again while Tumble flailed. The dog was growling. It was biting—

"Your dress!" Blue shouted as realization struck him. "It's going for your dress!"

Tumble was in too much of a state to hear him. Her legs were protected by the boots, but she kept swatting at the dog, putting her hands dangerously close to its teeth.

Blue plunged into the battle.

Tumble reached for his hand, but he grabbed a handful of yellow ruffles instead and yanked. A seam ripped, and he came away with a wad of fabric.

"Here, dog!" he said, waving it wildly at the animal, hoping his spur of the moment plan didn't get them both mauled. "Here!"

He threw the ruffles as hard as he could, and the dog spun away from Tumble to attack the strips of cloth lying on the road.

Tumble caught on fast. She was on her feet in an instant, tearing more lace and ruffles off the bottom of her dress and throwing them at the dog.

"You're really cursed!" she said with every rip. "You're extremely cursed! You are!"

"I know," Blue gasped, watching the dog cautiously.

It was demolishing the dress.

"This is crazy!" Tumble's voice had gone shrill.

"I *know*," said Blue.

Tumble clutched a stitch in her side with both hands and stared at the dog. It finished vanquishing the ruffles and started kicking dirt over the remains, looking pleased with itself.

"And I won the stupid race! This is unacceptable. It's not right." Tumble panted. "We have to fix this."

"I don't think there's a sewing machine on earth that can fix this."

"Not the dress, Blue! You! You're really-for-real cursed. We have to fix you."

He blinked at her. "I thought we were already trying to?"

Tumble coughed. "Right. We were. But now we're trying way, way harder."

"Kids!" called a breathless voice behind them. "Kids, are y'all all right? Beast, get back here right now!"

The dog, wagging its tail like it was a normal and well-adjusted member of canine society, trotted over to the man.

He was wearing a pale green shirt so drenched with sweat that it looked like he'd gone for a swim. His round face was frightened and red, and he was wheezing for air. He grabbed Beast's collar in both hands and held on so tightly that the dog's front feet lifted off the ground.

Beast tried to lick his face.

"Are you two okay? Did he hurt you?"

Then he saw Blue's injured leg, which was bloody from

knee to ankle after his frantic run. His eyes bugged. "Good night! Son, you need to sit down right now. You could pass out! I'm going to call an ambulance, or . . . no that'll take too long," he babbled. "You just wait here, just wait here and I'll get help and . . . Miss, you sit with him. I'm so sorry. I'll be right back. Right back!"

"The dog didn't get my leg," Blue said quickly.

"No, it was just my dress," said Tumble.

"The blood's from earlier."

"There was a deer."

"And *then* the dog."

"But I'm wearing snake boots so my legs are fine," Tumble added.

Blue had never seen a person look half as confused as the man did then.

"I don't need to go to the hospital because of a dog bite," he tried to explain. "I got trampled by a deer, though, and I probably need stitches. I was just at the emergency room last night, too."

"He almost blinded himself playing tiddlywinks," Tumble offered.

The stranger was still blinking at them.

Blue wiped the sweat off of his forehead with the back of his good arm. "Uh, I'm a Montgomery?"

"Oh!" said the man, relief making him loosen his grip on Beast's collar. "Oh . . . well. That explains it."

EIGHTEEN

THE RV PRINCE

The next day it rained, hard and fast, and Tumble spent the morning dashing around the house with pots and pans to catch drips. After lunch, she stood in the hallway with her parents, watching a brown stain ooze its way across the ceiling.

"I can fix it," her mother said with a sigh.

Tumble passed her a casserole dish.

Her mother stared through the dish's glass bottom. "I was going to use this for brownies when we visit Mr. Goat."

"I don't think you're supposed to call him Mr. Goat," Tumble's dad replied. He had somehow managed to find another dry towel. He tossed it onto the carpet to soak up the wet. "I think it's just Goat. Like Cher! But less well known."

"I refuse to call a grown man Goat."

"Well, I'm going to call him Goat," said Tumble. "He told me to."

The name wasn't exactly classy, like Tumble or Maximal Star, but it showed an individual nature.

"I think it shows an individual nature," she announced.

Her mother rolled her eyes. "You would."

Tumble was grateful to Goat for not mentioning that the Montgomerys were *special* when he was explaining to her parents what had happened. It turned out that Beast was their landlord's infamous curtain-eating dog. He'd been left in Goat's care when Mr. Patty moved, and he was the one who'd startled the deer.

"He just took off running after it, ma'am," Goat had said to Tumble's mother. "I was trying to call him back, but I guess he caught sight of Blue Montgomery and your girl having a footrace. And that dress—all I can figure is it reminded him of the drapes. I can't think of any other explanation."

He'd held a hand to his chest.

"The old ticker nearly jumped right out of me today when I was trying to catch him."

To apologize, Goat had invited them over to his cabin for dinner. Tumble's parents had been too baffled to refuse.

The stain on the ceiling dripped a drop of water onto Tumble's head, and her mother groaned. "So much for brownies."

She set the casserole dish on the floor.

"At least Tumble's made a friend," her dad said. "It sounds like Blue's a brave kid. He tried to save our daughter from a curtain-killer."

"I just wish he hadn't gotten hurt right after they met," her mother said. "What will his family think?"

"It's not like I kicked him in the leg or anything!" Tumble protested.

"It was a freak accident." Her dad smiled at her. "That's all."

"That's right," said Tumble, crossing her fingers behind her back. "That is completely correct."

By five o'clock that afternoon, the Wilsons were dressed and ready to go, even though it was too early.

"I'll get the television situation worked out soon," Tumble's dad promised as they stood around wondering what they were supposed to do. Listening to water splash into pans wasn't much entertainment.

"I could read aloud to you both," Tumble suggested.

Her mother smiled. "Lily, that sounds like a wonder—"

"Great! I'm on Chapter Thirteen again," Tumble said. "Maximal Star's about to save a guy from falling off a skyscraper."

Her mother flinched as if she'd been jabbed with a pin.

Tumble pulled her paperback copy of *How to Hero Every Day* out of her emergency backpack. The pack was filled with her first aid kit and a few other essentials that Maximal recommended. With Blue as a friend, Tumble had decided it would be best to keep it with her at all times.

"It's a great rescue. Maximal does it with nothing but a pair of long johns and a stapler."

"That sounds even more . . . unique than the last one you told us about," her mother said.

"It's amazing," her father added, "how old Maximal manages to always be in the right place at the right time to save people in such . . . unique ways."

"That might be how it seems to the layperson," Tumble explained. "But it's really all to do with Tenets Three and Twenty-Seven."

She waited for them to ask, but they didn't.

"The third Tenet of Heroism is 'Ever vigilant,'" she explained. "And Twenty-Seven is 'Creative in the absence of resources.'"

"You know what?" her mother said suddenly. "I just remembered I wanted to show you something on the porch."

"Huh?"

"On the porch. We can sit and watch the rain, and I'll show you something neat."

Tumble had seen the porch. Some of the boards had buckled. It was not neat. "But what about Tenet Twenty-Seven and the stapler?" she said to her parents' retreating backs.

The screen door squealed open.

Oh well. Tumble would convince them one day. She tucked the book carefully back into her bag beside a laminated sheet that showed the proper way to perform the Heimlich maneuver. Then she headed outside to find them both looking up at the porch's ceiling.

"See where the paint's flaked off?" Her mother was pointing to a corner where the gray paint was chipping.

"It's blue underneath," said her father.

Tumble saw that he was right. Beneath the gray, there was another layer of bright bluish paint.

Tumble considered the color. "It's pretty."

"I just thought it was interesting," her mother said. "This house had a feisty personality once. You don't get this kind of character with an RV."

Tumble thought that being able to travel all over the country was a more than decent trade-off for character. And the RV was fire-engine red. If that didn't show feistiness, she didn't know what did.

"But you don't *like* houses," Tumble said. "That's why we have the RV."

She didn't mean to let her tongue get ahead of her, but when you spent so much time thinking about something, it was hard to hold it in.

Her dad tilted his head. "What gave you that idea?" he asked. "It's not that we don't like houses. It's that . . . sometimes being in one place is harder."

Her mother nodded. "It can be tough when the situation changes around you, and you're stuck in the same rut, doing the same things."

Tumble's parents looked at each other, and she saw that they were remembering. All the way back to before Tumble. Before Lily. Before she was anyone at all.

"Are you thinking about Jason?" His name felt strange in her mouth, like a secret even though it wasn't quite.

Her mother cleared her throat. "Maybe a little, sweetheart."

Tumble clutched at her pocket. She could feel the plastic snack bag, always there. And with it, the outline of the picture. The pencil. The eraser.

"I . . ." But the words still weren't ready. They weren't right.

"Anyway," her dad said, "it would've broken your Grandpa Laffy's heart if we didn't want to roam around in one of his RVs."

"True." Her mother rested her hand against his arm. "Although I think he misses having me run the repairs department."

"You were the queen of Laffy Motors," he replied. "I

always felt like the court jester when I went to visit you there."

Tumble could see the little golden crown medallion gleaming on the side of the RV from here. "Come to Laffy's RV kingdom!" her grandpa's commercials said.

She hadn't considered how Grandpa Laffy fit into all this. Until now. Had her brother been there, running around Laffy Motors, being the kingdom's prince? Would Tumble have been an RV princess in another life?

Tumble wanted to demand answers. She wanted to apologize. But she couldn't do either.

At least not yet.

Oh, Maximal Star, she thought. *I wish you'd written a book on how to hero as fast as possible.*

NINETEEN

THE FLATS

At six, Eve Montgomery's Thunderbird pulled into the Wilsons' front yard, and Blue's grandmother splashed across the grass to offer them a spare umbrella. "It's gonna be a tight fit," she apologized. "Goat didn't invite Ma Myrtle, but I've been wanting to get her away from all the . . . well . . . you know."

Tumble's parents *didn't* know, and Tumble wasn't about to tell them.

Goat's house was only a couple of miles away. Blue's grandmother turned off the dirt road onto a private trail that was blocked by a gate covered in POSTED NO TRESPASSING signs.

Eve jumped out of the car and opened it. When she made it back, she was shaking rainwater out of her hair.

"I could've done that," said Blue. He waved his right arm at the rearview mirror.

"Hey!" said Tumble. "Your cast is off! That's great."

"You're not supposed to get your stitches wet," Eve said. "And I'm not sweet enough to melt."

Blue grinned at Tumble. "They took my cast off at the ER, but now my leg looks all Frankensteined." He leaned over and lifted the bandage so that he could show her the black stitches running up and down his bruised shin.

"How many are there?" Tumble asked. She was sardined between her parents, so she couldn't see as well as she would have liked.

"Thirty-nine."

"Impressive."

Goat's cabin wasn't what Tumble had expected. "Cabin" made the place sound like it would be built out of logs, but it was just a regular single-wide with yellow vinyl siding. A wooden deck built onto the back overlooked a creek.

She also spied a brand-new kennel with a Dogloo in it. Beast was probably hiding from the rain in there, but she was still glad she'd made a point of not wearing a single ruffle or frill.

"Hey, he's got a boat," said Blue, pointing toward a short dock where a green jon boat was tied.

"The outboard motor's been broken for months," Eve said.

Goat stepped out of his front door as she parked the car. He was holding a magazine over his head to block the rain and waving so enthusiastically that Tumble couldn't help but wave back.

Blue waited to help Ma Myrtle up the steps, so he was the last to enter Goat's house.

A teenage girl with bushy hair and glasses met him at the door. She was wearing tight jeans and pink high heels, and she was holding a box of double-decker chocolate MoonPies out in front of her like an offering.

"Hi," said Blue, shaking raindrops off his umbrella.

"Where's . . ." The girl craned her neck to see over Blue's shoulder.

"I'm the last one."

"But I thought . . . Howard's not with y'all?"

"No?"

"Oh." She pulled the MoonPies out of Blue's reach. "Uncle Goat said a Montgomery boy was coming, and I—"

"I'm Blue."

"Howard's back at home, Millie," said Granny Eve. She nodded at the box of snack cakes. "Are those for him?"

"No!" she said. "I mean yes. But only because I know he likes them. It can be for you instead, or you can give it to . . . or . . . here!" She turned bright red and practically threw the MoonPies at Blue.

"I'll give them to him," he promised.

"I'm just here to help Uncle Goat with the dinner is all," she muttered.

"You helped cook tonight?" Tumble's mother asked, sniffing the air. "It smells wonderful."

Millie nodded. "My parents own Flat's Restaurant. You should come try our famous swamp cakes. I'm there most days in the summer."

"How *is* Bagget?" Ma Myrtle asked, her eyes narrowed.

Bagget Flat was the one who'd fed Ma Myrtle bad deviled eggs, Blue realized. He hoped his great-grandmother wasn't going to mention the food poisoning in front of Mr. Flat's family.

"Daddy's the same as always," said Millie. "Cooking up a storm for the restaurant."

"All of us Flats cook," said Goat, waving them toward a pair of card tables that had been pushed together in the kitchen. "And eat!"

The whole group fit around the table, but only because nobody complained when they were bumped with an elbow or jostled with a shoulder. The Flats served sweet tea and Diet Coke, cheese grits and fried fish. A giant vegetarian lasagna filled the center of the table.

"For my ticker," Goat explained, loading his plate. "I'm trying to eat my vegetables."

Millie eventually recovered from her embarrassment. Over bowls full of cobbler for dessert, she told a story about how her father had stuffed himself with so much peach pie during an eat-off that the button on his pants had popped loose and left a dent in a spectator's forehead.

Goat burst into a laughing fit, and all at once, Blue understood why he was called goat.

"He *sounds* like a goat!" Tumble whispered. She sounded delighted.

"*Shhh* . . ." Blue said.

"I remember that!" Goat bleated, slapping the table so that the cobbler spoons rattled in their bowls. "Nobody's a better eater than my brother Bagget! When we were boys he nearly ran the restaurant out of business. He ate more of our swamp cakes than the customers did."

Ma Myrtle took that as a challenge. She slammed her tea glass down on the table. "Our Howard could eat a pie the size of Bagget himself if he had a mind to!"

Millie smiled dreamily. "It would impress Daddy if he did."

"Oh, it would!" said Goat. "It would impress him to no end. We ought to get Howard to come down to the restaurant and give it a try one of these days."

Ma Myrtle opened her mouth.

"He doesn't *do* eating contests," Blue said quickly. "Remember, Ma Myrtle?"

Ma Myrtle shot him a glare, but Blue didn't feel guilty. It was Ma Myrtle's fault that Howard's home was full of bloodthirsty Montgomerys. And with the way she was enjoying the chaos, Blue suspected that she would keep the relatives hanging around and fighting among themselves for a long while. The least she could do was not force Blue's cousin into battle with another famous eater.

TWENTY

THE OTHER
HALF

Tumble was stuffed. After dinner, when the adults dragged extra chairs into the living room, she plopped down onto the shag carpet beside Blue and tried hard not to burp.

Ma Myrtle and Eve took seats on the short sofa behind them. Her parents and Millie sat across from them on kitchen chairs. Goat, in an armchair that had to be almost as old as the man himself, was telling Tumble's dad that he was in charge of catching all the fish for Flat's Restaurant.

"How do you do that if your boat is broken?" Blue asked.

"I've still got my canoe," said Goat. "I keep it for when I want to head into the Okefenokee. Too tricky to get the jon boat down that way."

"Luna Montgomery," Ma Myrtle interrupted, "was a famous navigator. She sailed around the world on a raft she built out of coconut shells."

Eve sighed. "I don't think that's true, Mama."

"How would you know? I'm the only one who's read the family history." She tossed a strand of wispy gray hair over her shoulder and lifted her chin toward Tumble's parents. "Howard may not use his gifts, but others in our family are very talented. Right now, in fact, I've gathered them all together to show—"

"I want to hear more about fishing!" Tumble said. Her parents would be out the door in a flash if the Montgomerys started talking about fates and curses tonight.

"Mama, let's not tell family stories," Eve added. "The Wilsons have just moved here. We don't want to put *too much* on them at once."

"Nonsense, Evie. We should show them a Montgomery in action!" Ma Myrtle's skinny fingers flashed down to the space between the sofa's cushions and reappeared with a remote control.

"I've been looking everywhere for that!" Goat

slapped his knee and let out one of his bleating laughs.

"The show that comes on before our Samantha's is about to end." Ma Myrtle clicked the television on. She smiled mildly at the Wilsons. "My granddaughter Samantha has chosen not to visit me before my demise. But I do love her show anyway."

"Mama," Eve hissed. "They don't want to sit here all night watching Samantha's show. I thought it would be nice if the two of us had an evening *away* from the chaos, but if you can't behave—"

"Here it is!"

Tumble recognized the show that was coming on. It was a sitcom that she hadn't watched often, but she knew it was popular. And the main actress's name was—

"Samantha Lewis is related to you!" Tumble's dad exclaimed, leaning so far forward that his chair tipped.

Eve sighed. "Lewis was my fourth husband's name. She's not as charming in person, I'm afraid."

The show started with a tinkle of music, and Samantha appeared on the screen. She looked like a female version of Howard—dark hair and olive skin. Which

made sense when Blue told Tumble in a low whisper
that the actress was Howard's mother and that it was a
very sore subject.

Tumble wondered what it must be like to see a mother
you didn't know in real life on television every day.

When the first commercial break came, Eve spoke up.
"All right, that's enough, Mama," she said over the sound
of an advertisement for laundry detergent. She reached
for the remote.

Ma Myrtle tried to hold it out of the way, but Eve
snagged it and peered down at the buttons.

"Goat doesn't want us filling up his living room until
kingdom come," she said. "And I'm sure the Wilsons
need to be getting home."

"That would be best," Tumble's mother agreed. "We've
got a few leaks, and we don't want the pans to overflow
onto the floor."

"I can put you in touch with a roofer," Goat offered.

"Thank you, but I like to do my own repairs."

"Where's the off switch on this thing, Goat?" said Eve.

Tumble pushed herself up onto her knees to help Blue's

grandmother find the right button. Suddenly, from his chair across the room, her father said, "No, don't turn it off!"

Tumble looked at him. He was gesturing toward the television.

"We've got a little fame in our own family," he said. "Look, Tumble! It's Grandpa Laffy's commercial."

A bus-sized RV—the same model as their family's—rolled across the screen. Light flashed off its chrome. It's crown emblem twinkled. And then Grandpa Laffy was there, wearing purple velvet and ermine like the monarch in a school play. He even had a scepter made out of a hood ornament.

"Come to Laffy's RV Kingdom today!" the announcer's voice boomed.

"And you'll be ruling the roads tomorrow," Tumble and her parents said. They were perfectly in time with the announcer.

"Grandpa Laffy really needs to get a new commercial," said Tumble, turning back to help Eve with the remote. "He should have you write a jingle for it, Dad."

"Grandpa Laffy?" Ma Myrtle said.

"It's this button, Mrs. Eve," said Tumble, pointing.

But Eve's fingers had stopped moving. She was staring at Tumble, then at Ma Myrtle, and then back again. Her head was moving so quickly that she looked like she was trying to work a cramp out of her neck.

"*Grandpa* Laffy?!" Ma Myrtle said, much more shrilly this time. "That's old Deirdre LaFayette's boy!"

"Oh!" Tumble's mother sounded delighted. "Did you know my grandmother?"

"Ma Myrtle," said Goat, standing up, "are you all right?"

Ma Myrtle was clutching the front of her blouse in both of her wrinkled hands. "LaFayettes! LaFayettes are among us! That's how it all goes wrong!"

"Mama!" Eve said sharply. "Don't be ugly."

"Bedevilment!" wailed Ma Myrtle, falling back into the cushions. "Ill fortune in my final days!"

Tumble felt someone tugging on the sleeve of her shirt, and she turned to see Blue, his wide eyes matching her own.

"What's going on?" she said.

He shook his head. "I don't exactly—"

Eve stood. "Mama, we are not going to do this here in front of these nice people!"

Tumble's parents were staring at Ma Myrtle with alarm. "Is she okay?" Tumble's father asked.

Eve smiled at them. "Don't worry, please. Ma Myrtle is just a little excitable. A little histrionic."

"Does she need—"

"To go," Eve said, pulling her mother onto her feet by one arm. "She'll feel better when she gets back to the house. She's enjoying the company of our . . . beloved relations."

Ma Myrtle and Eve glared at each other for a tense moment. Then Ma Myrtle snatched her arm away, and with a last dark look at the Wilsons, she marched out of the room.

By the time the door slammed, Eve was already smoothing things over. "Her health, you know. And she doesn't quite know how to deal with everything that's happening right now. . . ."

Tumble's mother was nodding sympathetically, but Tumble still felt completely baffled.

"What's wrong with LaFayettes?" she whispered to Blue. "Grandpa Laffy's just as friendly as anyone."

He stood and stretched. "I'm going to make sure Ma Myrtle's not too upset," he said, but he dropped his arms and made a follow-me gesture behind his back.

Tumble trailed behind him into the kitchen and out onto Goat's front steps. It was still drizzling outside but not as badly as it had been. Ma Myrtle was already back in the car.

"What on earth was that about?"

Blue's face scrunched. "You remember the story I told you? About my family, and the golden alligator? Munch?"

Tumble snorted. "It's kind of hard to forget something like that."

"Well, I should have told you more." He frowned down at his arm. It looked pale and thin without its cast on it. "I should have told you the other half of the story."

There's more? thought Tumble. How much stranger could the Montgomerys get?

"What's the other half?"

"The LaFayettes are," said Blue, looking back up at her. "*You* are."

How very human of Blue to forget Almira.

Her likeness was carved into the wood over their front door, but the Montgomerys preferred to treat her as a side character. When the story was passed down, she was little more than an explanation.

A woman named LaFayette had ruined it all under the red moon, they said. She was why everything had gone sideways.

A partial truth. The worst kind of lie because it slides so smoothly down the gullet.

Here is what actually happened that night. Swallow with care. You'll find my version has had none of its sharp edges removed.

Red everywhere.

Overhead, dripping from the sickle moon. Underfoot, staining the leaves. Sparkling on the surface of the black water.

Red filled the whites of Walcott's eyes. It dried in the curved spaces beneath Almira's fingernails.

The sounds were almost animal. Crack of bone. Shriek and thud. And that old, familiar smell on the air, mingling with the blood.

"Do you know what humans smell like?" I said, when the battle paused. "Under the skin, behind the veins?"

Greed.

Their faces, twisted with exhaustion and pain, were growing brighter. The red was falling away from the moon.

"Do continue," I said. "You're almost out of time."

They stood facing each other, chests lifting and lowering, until finally Walcott spoke in that mosquito-whine of a voice.

"We'll kill each other at this rate. Is that what you want, you dark thing?"

A question only a human would ask. Under the red moon, I do not *want*. I am.

"Can't we split it?" Almira said suddenly, wiping red from her mouth. "You could break it in two."

A bad idea.

I told them. I explained, oh so clearly, what a broken fate would mean for the Montgomerys and LaFayettes who came after them.

"But would we have what *we* want?" Walcott asked. He spat a tooth on the ground. "Would we have the luck?"

Yes. They would.

"Well! That's it then. That's all I care about," said Walcott.

And Almira agreed.

So for the first time in history, I broke a great fate in half. And I knew how it would sink its claws into human after human, on down through the years, all the way to Tumble and to Blue. Every death, every hurt, every broken arm and stitched shin—I knew on that very night.

And you're wrong. I'm not the monster.

All I am is true.

TWENTY-ONE

FATE
FREE

Tumble burrowed deeper under her fuzzy blanket and tried to remember everything Maximal Star had ever said about *feeling* like a hero.

Nothing. Nothing at all.

Apparently, he had never had a crisis of confidence before. Or maybe he hadn't written about it.

Tumble latched on to this idea and refused to let go. All heroes probably had doubts sometimes, she told herself. If she ever met Maximal Star, she would mention that he ought to write about the parts in between the daring rescues. The parts where you felt like a big-time faker and a failure.

The other half of the story.

Tumble didn't want to be the other half of the Montgomerys' story. She had already been feeling a little—just a tad—overwhelmed by the idea of helping Blue deal with his fate.

She didn't want one of her own to contend with, too.

Blue didn't understand why she was upset. "You've got one of the *good* ones," he'd whispered to her while Mrs. Eve was saying good-bye to her parents. "Tumble, your *heroing stuff*—that's your talent. You really are a hero."

And he'd looked at her so hopefully.

It was the best thing anyone had ever said to Tumble. She'd been waiting all this time for someone to think she could save them. So why couldn't she sleep?

Maybe it was the RV. Maybe it was just that the coconut shampoo smell was starting to fade.

Tumble did her breathing exercise. She counted her seconds over and over. But when the sunlight started to filter through the pleated shades, she hadn't gotten even a minute of sleep.

Laffy Motors and Maximal Star had failed her on the very same night.

Laffy Motors. Tumble's grandpa was an RV king. Was that all because of some talent? And her mother. What about Monica LaFayette Wilson? She was *normal*. No curses. No magical gifts.

Maybe it wears off, Tumble thought.

The idea made her sit right up in bed.

It. Wore. Off.

Of course it did! It had been *two hundred* years. Tumble had heard Ma Myrtle bragging about Montgomerys from the past who had so many powerful and terrible fates. But now they had people in the family like that Ernestine girl, who almost wasn't cursed at all. She made lights flicker. What kind of a dreadful burden was *that*?

Maybe Almira LaFayette had gotten a smaller dose of whatever strange magic went on in the swamp that night. Maybe Tumble and her mother were fate free. And even if they weren't, they must have such small talents that they hadn't even noticed them.

Tumble was probably great at painting with her toes, or playing the glockenspiel, or something else she'd never tried.

Fate free! That's me.

She hoped Blue was awake. She had to tell him that

she was only a regular hero. Not a *destined* one. And she was still in training, after all. He needed to understand that.

Tumble raced out of the RV and into the house to get dressed, but when she reached the hallway, she was assaulted by a chokingly sour smell. And when her bare feet touched the hall carpet, it squished.

"Eeew!" Cold water oozed up around her toes.

She shoved the RV keys into the pocket of her pajama shorts and tiptoed as fast as she could to her parents' room. "Mom. Daddy. You guys! The carpet has gone funky."

Her father fumbled for the switch on the reading lamp by the bed. He clicked it on, and in the yellow light, Tumble saw his face cringe as he rolled out of bed and his feet hit the floor.

"Wow, that's no way to wake up."

"And it *reeks*," said Tumble. "What are we going to do?"

Instead of having breakfast, they spent the morning pulling up the mildewing carpet.

"Yuuuuuck," Tumble said as she scooped handfuls of squishy, drippy carpet backing into a plastic bucket. "Why can't we go back to the RV? This house is a *dump*."

Her mother was on her hands and knees at the other end of the hall with her own plastic bucket. "Lily, I swear if you mention the RV one more time before your dad gets back from the hardware store—"

So Tumble didn't mention it, but she thought about it. She thought about how the RV didn't have carpet. The RV didn't leak. The RV smelled like leather seats and coconut shampoo. And her parents were making her live in this house, which was probably a biohazard now, when the RV was parked *right outside*.

Tumble was working herself into a state over the wrongness and insanity of her whole life, throwing chunks of rotten carpet at the overflowing bucket with increasing rage, when Blue's voice came from the front of the house.

"Hello? Is anybody here?"

They'd left the door open, trying to air out the stench.

Tumble's mother looked up. "Fine," she said, wiping her frustrated, sweaty face on the collar of her T-shirt.

"Fine. Go with him and don't come back until your attitude's improved."

Tumble didn't need telling twice. She abandoned her bucket and raced to the screen door.

Blue was standing on the other side of it, his nose wrinkling. "Something smells weird."

"We've flooded," said Tumble. She joined him on the porch. "And I don't have any superpowers. I'll explain it all on the way to your house."

TWENTY-TWO

OPPOSITES

To Blue's delight, Tumble became a regular at the Montgomery house as May turned into June.

She still wouldn't admit to having a fate of her own, but Blue knew better. Even if Tumble's talent wasn't heroism, there would be something else. Sometimes it took a while for people to figure their fates out. It had taken his grandmother decades.

In the meantime, Tumble had called a temporary halt to their attempts to turn him into a winner. She wanted to work out a truly foolproof plan this time.

"It's no good if you die trying to beat fate. You've damaged an eye and a leg already." She set her jaw. "Next time, nobody's getting hurt."

"'Caution keeps away casualties'?" said Blue.

"You're reading the book!" Tumble whooped and punched his shoulder. "That's from Chapter One!"

Blue wasn't sure how much further he could stand to go in *How to Hero Every Day*. Even though Maximal Star's advice seemed okay, his stories were a little *too* amazing. But he wasn't about to tell Tumble that.

While they waited for the foolproof plan to come out of hiding, the two of them kept a close eye on the other Montgomerys, timed themselves running up and down the road, and tried to make the attic more livable.

One morning, Tumble found a vent hidden under one of the boxes, and when they opened it, cool wind blew their hair out of their faces.

"Air-conditioning!" said Tumble.

Shifting yet another mountain of cardboard revealed a carving. It was on the wall opposite the window, and they had to crouch under the low roof to get a good look at it. It was smaller than the one over the front door of the house, and instead of two people shaking hands, it showed only Almira LaFayette.

Her face was harsh, with a sharp triangle for a nose. She was standing in a patch of reeds. The word FOLLOW was carved into them. Two crescent moons had been cut into the wood, one above her head and another beneath the reeds. Almira was pointing at the bottom one.

"That's weird," said Blue. "Why is it just her?"

"Why are there two moons?" Tumble traced the carving with her finger.

Hidden in the attic, the image felt like a clue.

Just not one they needed. Some of the other Montgomerys had already guessed that following the red sickle moon was part of the trick—like chasing a rainbow to a pot of gold at the end. But Ma Myrtle swore there was more to it than that, so the battle for her approval was still on.

Telescopes dotted the backyard now, courtesy of relatives who were hoping to spot the faintest hint of crimson on the moon.

"Waning crescent moons for three more days," Blue told Tumble. He'd gotten very good at reading the lunar calendars scattered throughout the house. "Then the new moon, then waxing crescents for a few more days. And then no more crescent moons until the very end of the month. After . . ."

"After Ma Myrtle's gone," said Tumble.

Blue nodded.

"You *do* think Ma Myrtle will tell someone how to get the new fate, don't you? Before she dies?"

"I think so," Blue said. "She's not evil . . . just . . . she'll draw it out, I think. To make sure none of them ever forget about her."

They would certainly never do that. As her death date approached, Ma Myrtle refused to slow down. There were late-night dancing contests. There were bake-offs instead of breakfasts. She'd even woken the whole house up once for a midnight poetry slam.

That afternoon, when she called all of the relatives out onto the porch to entertain her, Tumble and Blue took advantage of the rare chance to sit at the kitchen table without half a dozen Montgomerys surrounding them. They talked about ways to break Blue's fate, writing wild idea after wild idea down in the notebook Tumble had started to carry in her emergency backpack.

When Eve came in to get started on supper, she poured them each a glass of iced tea.

"Do y'all need a snack?" she asked, pulling a leftover Coca-Cola ham out of the refrigerator. "You can help yourselves to anything. I'm sending the twins to the grocery store again tomorrow."

The telephone rang.

Eve set the ham on the counter and stepped over to pluck the phone off the wall. "Hello?"

A second later, her free hand went to her hip. "Well!" she said. "Look who's decided to make time for the rest of us!"

Blue jumped up so quickly that his chair would have overturned if Tumble hadn't caught it.

His dad. It had to be. He had left so many messages, and his dad couldn't be *that* busy watching the races. He reached for the phone.

Eve used her elbow to nudge him back an inch so that she wouldn't be talking into his hair. "Yes, he's here," she said. "Yes, well enough, all things considered. But Alan, the way you've been behaving—"

"Dad!" Blue said loudly. "Hi, Dad! I'm right here."

Eve shot him a quelling look that did nothing to quell him. He was an instant away from trying to make another grab for the phone when she sighed and handed it to him.

"Dad," said Blue. "Hey!"

"Hi there, Skeeter." It sounded almost like his dad was calling him from a swimming pool. Blue could hear splashing in the background. And lots of voices. "Sorry I haven't called in a few days. Just busy with things over here."

"What things?"

"Racing. All of it. You know."

Blue didn't. Not really. But at least they were talking. "I got my cast off."

"Hey!" said his dad. "I forgot that was coming up. Way to go! How's the arm?"

"Good. It's nice that it doesn't itch anymore."

"Glad to hear it. You'll be back to your old self in no time."

Blue knew he didn't mean anything by it, but still . . . His old self? His not-good-enough self?

"About that," he said. "I think you'll be pretty surprised when you come to pick me up."

Twelve minutes, Blue thought. He ran to the sign every morning. He was getting faster, and usually Tumble kept him company. "I've made friends with the girl from next door—"

"Hi, Blue's dad!" Tumble shouted toward the phone.

Blue grinned. "That's her. And the two of us . . . we're working on my fate."

Eve had been getting a knife to cut up the Coca-Cola ham. She slammed the drawer with her backside and raised both eyebrows at Blue.

His dad's voice was suddenly uncomfortable. "I never asked you to—"

"No, it's good," said Blue. "By the time you get all of the racing stuff figured out, I'll be—"

"Is your granny listening in?" his dad demanded.

"She's cutting up a ham."

"I told you not to mention the racing to her!" he said, voice rising. "When I dropped you off, wasn't that one of the things I told you?"

He had. Blue had forgotten.

"I . . . sorry, I didn't mean to."

"Let me talk to her."

"No!" said Blue. He grabbed the old phone's spiraling cord as if it could hold his dad on the line. "Not yet. I needed to tell you—"

"Let me talk to her!"

"What are you so mad about?" Blue crushed the phone's cord in his hand. His eyes stung, but he wouldn't let them do more than that. Not in front of Tumble and his grandmother. "Why does it matter if Granny Eve knows?"

"Blue," his dad said. "I'm telling you I want to talk to your granny right now."

Blue breathed fast. He tried to understand why his dad was angry. It was such a little mistake.

"Granny Eve."

His grandmother was chopping the ham with a fury that implied the pig had done something to offend her. Tumble was watching them both wide-eyed, her glass of tea halfway to her mouth.

Blue swallowed to steady his voice. "Dad wants to talk to you."

His grandmother plunged the knife into the ham, and stomped over.

"You didn't do a thing wrong, Blue," she said in a crisp voice as she took the phone. "This is just an old pot that's finally decided to boil over."

Then into the phone, she said, "Alan, after what happened last time . . . how could you—?"

Her lips narrowed.

"Well, maybe you *don't* have to explain yourself to me. And you obviously won't explain yourself to your own boy." She drew in a long breath that pulled her shoulders back and made her chest swell. "So why don't you try talking *to your own darn self.*"

She slapped the phone back onto the wall.

Blue took a step back.

Eve was glaring at the phone as if daring it to ring.

Tumble set her glass on the table. "Hey!" she said in a strained voice. "Hey, Blue! Let's go upstairs. I've just had the best idea about that carving up there!"

Tumble hadn't had any kind of an idea about the carving, but she would make something up when they reached the attic. She talked as fast as she could all the way upstairs, hoping to distract Blue from whatever had gone wrong. She had been able to hear Blue's dad *shouting* at him, though not well enough to understand what he was saying. And his grandmother . . .

Tumble had never seen her that mad. Not even when the relatives spilled green paint down the grand staircase.

Not even when someone threw a croquet mallet through one of the windows.

So Tumble was rambling on and on about Maximal Star. And she was thinking how unfair it was that someone like Maximal couldn't be born with a powerful gift and someone like Blue's dad could, when the answer they'd been looking for all this time hit her like a croquet mallet to the head.

She actually tripped. If Blue hadn't grabbed the back of her T-shirt, she would have smashed her face into the attic steps.

"Are you okay?"

He sounded deflated to Tumble. And defeated. Defeat was the most dangerous emotion during a crisis, and Tumble didn't have time for it.

She shook him off and dashed up the last few stairs, excitement making her floaty. She spun around when she reached the top, and looked down at him with her arms spread wide. "Blue, I've got it! Opposites!"

"What?"

"The Montgomery fates . . . some of them are *opposites*."

He blinked up at her.

"Your dad *wins*," Tumble said impatiently. "You *lose*."

"I know." Blue's shoulders slumped.

"Blue!" She flapped her arms at him. "Don't you get it? What would happen if you and your dad were a *team*?"

TWENTY-THREE

FLAT AS A FLITTER

Opposite fates. It was an idea so perfect Blue couldn't believe he'd never thought of it before. What would happen if a winner and a loser worked together?

Unfortunately, with his dad out of reach, Tumble and Blue needed a different pair of opposites to test their theory. That was why they volunteered to help the twins buy groceries the next afternoon.

On the way into town, they shared the backseat of the twins' car with Howard, who'd come along after swearing he would commit murder if he had to pretend to get along with the other Montgomerys for one more minute.

"*Have* you been pretending?" Ida asked as Jenna turned the car onto Main Street. "Wow. You're really bad at it."

"They're a bunch of backstabbing buzzards. Do you know someone's drawn a countdown on the shower curtain in one of the second-floor bathrooms? I tried to wash it off, but it's in permanent marker."

"Another moon calendar?" asked Blue.

"No!" Howard spat the word. "It's a countdown to when Ma Myrtle dies. I'm mad at her, but that's *disgusting*. What if she sees it? What if Granny Eve sees it!"

He kicked the back of Ida's seat.

"Howard!"

"Most of these people don't even *know* her. Or us! They've never bothered to talk to us before in their lives. Their grandparents ran away from Murky Branch generations ago."

"And they're trashing our house," Jenna said grimly.

Ida sighed. "What do you two want to do about it? We're already spying on them and plotting against them. Are we supposed to poison the groceries, too?"

She was joking, but Howard and Jenna didn't laugh.

"I'm pretty sure I'm not allowed to poison anyone," Tumble said.

"It's just one summer. Maybe only a few more days. We can do this. And then they'll be gone."

"Tumble and I've got an idea," said Blue. "One that will make them be gone *faster*."

He bumped Tumble's elbow.

"That's right," she said. "It's a perfect plan. You're going to love it."

"It'll change your lives," Blue added.

Jenna glanced at them in the rearview mirror. "Oh yeah? Well, if it's life-changing, save it for lunch. I'm starving."

A moment later, she drove the car into the parking lot of Flat's Restaurant.

"Wait." Howard's eyes widened. "We're supposed to be going to the grocery store!"

"It's one o'clock. I don't want to drive all that way on an empty stomach." She parked them beside a truck covered in mud and Gone Fishing bumper stickers.

Howard sank so low into his seat, he looked like he was melting into the upholstery.

Ida turned around in her seat. "Howard," she said soothingly. "Millie Flat's a nice girl. She won't bite."

"Just try not to embarrass us all this time, Romeo," said Jenna.

Flat's Restaurant smelled like pancakes and french fries. It had a checkered tile floor that squeaked against the soles of Blue's flip-flops, and oldies music was playing on a radio next to the cash register. Millie Flat was on duty, and by the time Howard slunk into the restaurant, she had already seated the rest of them at a corner booth and passed out giant laminated menus.

The bell over the door tinkled as he came in, and Howard flinched like it was a siren.

"Howard!" Goat's niece practically sang his name.

She snatched the menu right out of Blue's hands and ran toward Howard, holding it out eagerly. But as soon as she reached him, red blotches spread across her cheeks and she stopped talking. Which was too bad, because Howard wasn't talking, either.

"That's so sweet," Ida whispered.

"But also annoying," said Jenna. "We'll probably never get to order at this rate."

When Howard and Millie finally made it back to the

table, Tumble was laughing into her hand and Blue was pretending to stare very hard at his menu.

Howard squeezed into the booth beside them. His forehead was sweating.

"Are you okay?" Blue asked after Millie took their orders and left.

"What's this great idea of yours?" Howard said in a croaky voice. "It sounded important. Really important."

"You're adorable," Jenna cooed.

The look Howard shot at her would have withered grass.

"Our idea actually *is* really important," Tumble said. "We know how to break your curse, Ida."

Blue's cousins stared at her.

"Tell them Blue."

He took a deep breath. "Have you ever noticed," he said, "that a lot of the Montgomery fates are opposites?"

By the time Millie brought their lunches, Ida was as green as a swamp cake.

"Flat as a flitter and twice as tasty!" Millie announced, sliding a stack of the famous pancakes toward Blue.

Tumble wondered how much food coloring it took to turn batter that particular shade of lime. "What's a flitter?" she asked as Millie passed her a bottle of dressing for her salad.

"Umm . . . a flat thing?" Millie shrugged. "My mama says it."

She seemed to have recovered her voice, but when she gave Howard his plate, she spilled a few baked beans down the front of her apron. She squeaked in horror and disappeared so quickly that they didn't even have time to ask for a refill on their drinks.

Jenna leaned so far across the table that the tip of her long braid trailed through the gravy on top of her mashed potatoes.

"Listen," she muttered to Blue, "I know you're upset about your dad and being left here and being a los—"

"A long way from home," Ida said, her voice weak. "But that's no reason to suggest that I . . . that we . . . gerbils are dangerous! They eat their wounded. Everyone knows that."

Howard was looking thoughtfully down at his beans. "It could work."

"No it couldn't!"

"It makes sense," Howard insisted. "We should have thought of it years ago."

Ida shook her head. "I don't even want to talk about it. I don't want the gerbils to know."

"The Gerbellion are at home in their habitats right now, Ida," Jenna said, annoyance creeping into her voice. "They're not going to *get* you."

Ida pulled her knees to her chest as if she thought the gerbils might be scurrying around Flat's Restaurant. "They want to, though," she said darkly. "They always want to. When you're not in the room they line up along the glass and press their awful little paws against it, and they stare and stare and stare."

"Oh, they do not!" said Jenna. "The whole reason I have gerbils is that they're not aggressive. And I've been training these for ages. They haven't bitten you once!"

Tumble perched her fork on the edge of her plate. "That's perfect," she said. "Don't you see? We have *friendly, trained* gerbils who love you, Jenna."

"And we have Ida, who the friendly, trained gerbils hate," Blue added.

"So if we put the two of you together—"

"And then we make the gerbils choose whether to obey Jenna or snack on Ida—"

"Someone has to lose!" Tumble and Blue said together.

The twins exchanged identical, doubtful frowns.

Tumble decided it was time to sweeten the deal. "And you've got to think about Ma Myrtle. She wants someone to impress her, right? To show they're brave enough and smart enough to make it in the swamp? Well . . . this would be really brave of you, Ida. And breaking your curse would *prove* you're smarter than any Montgomery *ever*. Blue and I won't take any credit. We'll say the idea was all yours."

Howard was nodding now. "Who cares about the stupid alligator?" he said. "If we could break our curses we might not need to go into the swamp at all."

"What about Granny Eve?" Jenna said.

"What if breaking one curse broke *all* of them?" Howard countered.

The words zinged through the air. Tumble and Blue had already thought it, even though they were trying not to be too hopeful.

Tumble nodded at Howard. "Either way," she said, "you won't lose."

Blue cleared his throat. "That's right," he said. "Either the gerbils will have to be nice to you, Ida. Or they'll have to disobey Jenna. Someone's fate is going to change, and that's something even Ma Myrtle can't ignore."

"I'll think about it," Ida whispered. Her voice was so quiet that they almost couldn't hear it over the sound of the radio.

Howard snorted. "What's there to think ab—"

"Eat your beans," Jenna snapped, sitting back in the booth and patting Ida on the arm. "She promised to think about it."

Then she pointed a spoon at Tumble and Blue. "I'm in if Ida is," she said. "But if my gerbils get hurt, I'll make sure every animal in the Okefenokee knows I don't like you."

TWENTY-FOUR

THE GRAND REVUE

B lue hung around the twins' room for almost an hour that night, hoping to convince Ida that she was their best and only chance. When Jenna finally tossed him out, he called through the door, "Maybe the gerbils can't tell the two of you apart! You're twins! Maybe they're color blind."

Jenna opened the door and pointed at him. "The Gerbellion know their own mother. Now GO TO BED."

She slammed it in his face.

"Harsh," said Howard. He had just come up the stairs, carrying a gallon jug full of chocolate milk under one brawny arm.

Instead of turning into his own room, he followed Blue up the steps to the third floor. "You're not allowed in the attic," Blue informed him with a glance back over his shoulder. "Since you won't share your room it's only fair."

"Hey, I helped clean the attic. Remember?"

"Your doorknob *electrocuted* me."

"You keep mentioning that," said Howard. He looked like he was holding back a grin. "I'm not going to the attic anyway. I'm heading to the bathroom. All of the other showers are full."

"Still?"

It's funny how you get used to things so quickly, he thought when they parted ways at the top of the stairs. Compared to everything else going on in the house, Howard drinking chocolate milk in the shower almost seemed ordinary.

That night, Blue couldn't turn his brain off.

He was excited about the plan he and Tumble had come up with, and he was upset that the phone call with his dad had gone wrong. His grandmother had been angry, just like his dad predicted. What was it she'd said?

After what happened last time.

Was she worried about accidents? Blue's dad had never been hurt. Alan Montgomery cruised right past wrecks on the track.

Blue rolled over and stared at the paint-splattered poster taped to its tower of boxes. He could hear the air conditioner blowing through the floor vent, and he could smell lemon cake from the last time he'd burned Ida's candle. He didn't feel so lonely up here, knowing that Tumble and his cousin had tried to make the place cheerful.

Finally, he closed his eyes and drifted off to sleep.

Slam.

Blue's eyes snapped open. At first, he wasn't sure what had woken him, but then the sound came again. And again. Banging noises were coming from downstairs.

As he listened, the sound moved up through the house. On the second story it was still muffled, but then it reached the third.

Blue rolled off his mattress and pressed his ear to the floorboards. He could hear a hinge shriek and then a slam. *Slam, slam.*

Voices were chattering, and there was a question in their tones that he couldn't quite make out.

Then he heard feet pounding down the stairs.

Blue was tempted to stay up in his attic and let whatever new madness this was go on without him, but then he reconsidered. What if some especially ill-fated cousin had caused a tornado to touch down? What if Greg the fire-starting guy had decided to sleep inside tonight, and now the house was in flames?

Blue threw off his sheets, grabbed his duffel bag, and hurried downstairs.

At first, he thought something must have happened to Ma Myrtle. Her time hadn't run out, but with every single person in the house trying to crowd into her bedroom, he couldn't imagine what else it might be.

But then, over the hubbub, Cousin Chelsea shouted so loudly that her hair rollers shook. "Quiet, y'all! Our darling, wise, and *beloved* matriarch is making the announcement."

The announcement? wondered Blue. She couldn't mean . . .

The Montgomerys pushed in closer, trampling on one another's bunny slippers, knocking eyeglasses off of faces and dental retainers out of mouths.

"Ma Myrtle, you look awfully young for a ninety-seven-year-old!"

They stood on top of a coiled garden hose to see what was happening inside. Ma Myrtle was there, standing on the seat of an armchair so that she could see over the pack of Montgomerys pressing in around her.

"Is she going to tell *everyone* how to find Munch?" Blue asked. He wondered if he should go get dressed. Or call Tumble. What if it was *tonight*? The moon was due to be a waning sickle according to the calendars, but it hadn't risen yet.

He shifted his weight on top of the hose and wished he could hear what was going on. "Can you open the window?"

"Maybe." Ida hunched over for a moment, and when she straightened, she had a garden trowel in her hand. "If it's not locked, I think I can. . . ."

She dug the tip of the trowel under the window, ignoring the fact that the metal was biting into the painted wood. When she had it in place, she balled up her fist and brought it down on the handle. Once, twice. The window lifted just enough for the two of them to make out the din from inside.

"By the way," said Ida, "watch out for bats. And opos-

"Did I tell you about how I'm going to name my f
born Myrtle? Boy or girl! It's such a gorgeous name

Blue dropped his bag and stood on his tiptoes, bu
couldn't catch a glimpse of his great-grandmother.

He did spot Howard in the middle of the group, pu
ing his way through the relatives. Nobody was movi
for him, but it didn't matter. He was using his bul
shoulders like battering rams, and he didn't mind thro
ing an elbow or two in the direction of the more terrib
family members.

Ida stumbled out of the crowd and into Blue. He
rainbow hair was sticking up in all directions, and he
purple pajamas were rumpled. "They shoved me righ
out of the room!"

Without waiting for a reply, she turned on her bare
heels and ran toward the entryway. Blue, hoping she had
a plan, followed. They dashed out the front door and
around the other side of the house. When they jumped
off the porch, the grass was wet with dew underfoot.

Blue didn't have long to wonder about where they
were going. Ida stopped just outside Ma Myrtle's bedroom window.

sums. And raccoons. Raccoons are the worst. I had to have rabies shots the last time one got me." She looked down at her feet. "And I didn't have time to put on my snake boots."

"I'll keep them away from you if I see any," Blue promised.

They listened as hard as they could, and finally, the relatives quieted enough for them to pick out Ma Myrtle's voice.

"I'm sure you don't like being woken at three in the morning," she said, holding a hand over her chest like she was pledging allegiance. "But I hope you will understand time runs differently for an old woman who is ringing death's doorbell."

"Oh, poor Granny Eve," breathed Ida.

Their grandmother was sitting on the foot of Ma Myrtle's bed. She looked pale and worn out.

"My dear Evie says I should stop holding the family in suspense," said Ma Myrtle. "She says it's time I do what I mean to do."

The room broke out in excited whispers.

"Well, that's the truth," Ida muttered.

Ma Myrtle held up a hand to quiet the relatives, then said into the silence. "In eighteen days . . ."

Blue was gripping the windowsill so tightly his knuckles hurt.

". . . you will all be a part of my Grand Revue!"

Eve looked at her sharply.

"What?" said Blue. Ida was trembling so hard he could feel the hose underneath them vibrating. "She's not telling us which crescent moon will be red? Or how to find the alligator? Or—"

Ma Myrtle lifted her arms into the air triumphantly. A couple of people clapped, but Blue could tell they didn't understand any better than he did.

Ma Myrtle's lips pursed. "The Grand Revue," she said, "will be a display of our family's many aptitudes. A day of merriment and mirth in honor of my life! It will stave off the sadness you will no doubt endure when I leave you."

"Oh, Granny Eve looks mad now," whispered Ida. "I think Ma Myrtle's changed the plan on her."

Blue was counting in his head. Eighteen days. Ma Myrtle was supposed to die in *nineteen* days.

"Dear, sweet Ma Myrtle," said Chelsea, hovering near her chair, "what *is* a Grand Revue?"

"It's another talent contest," Howard said, crossing his arms over his chest. "Of course."

Chelsea's face brightened at once. She was no doubt already planning a new lineup of songs and dances for her son.

"The *Grand Revue* is not a talent contest," Ma Myrtle said. "It is a festival. A celebration! A showcase of everything that makes this family great."

"Yep," said Howard. "It's a talent contest."

"At the *GRAND REVUE*," Ma Myrtle said, talking over him, "all of Murky Branch will witness what our family can do. And I will announce the name of the champion who has proved himself or herself worthy of a new fate!"

"Ida," said Blue.

His cousin turned to look at him. In the light from the window, he could see that she was close to tears.

"You've got to do it," he breathed. "Before the Revue."

"What?"

"It's the only way to convince her to call the whole thing off," Blue said. "If we can break your fate—"

Ida shook her head. "No. I told you I can't—"

"A Grand Revue?" said Blue. "In this family? People are going to end up burned and electrocuted and trampled and who knows what else!"

Ida bit her lip. "And . . . it will keep all of the relatives here for weeks. When all Granny Eve wants is some time alone with her mother."

Blue hadn't quite thought of it that way. But Ida was right. Granny Eve must want a chance to say good-bye to Ma Myrtle.

"We can do this," he said, watching her with bated breath. "I know we can."

"You say we," she murmured at last, "but what you really mean is *me*."

"You'll do it?"

She slumped against the wall of the house and sighed. "I really hate gerbils."

TWENTY-FIVE

WAITING

The next few days were a blur of activity.

Invitations went out to everyone in Murky Branch, welcoming them to attend Ma Myrtle's Grand Revue. It would, the invitations said, include live music, a poetry recital, fireworks, victuals, a three-legged race, and a swamp cake–eating contest. Among other entertainments. The general consensus in town was that it would be a catastrophe, and also the most spectacular event of the year.

Tumble had encouraged Ma Myrtle to include the swamp cake contest. If Operation Gerbellion failed, then Howard would be their last chance.

"All he has to do is beat Bagget Flat at eating his own famous swamp cakes. Ma Myrtle will love it, and she'll tell Howard how to find the alligator. Then he can tell your grandmother, and that will be something at least."

Blue thought it was a good idea. The twins were happy to have a backup plan. All of them agreed that it was only fair for Howard to contribute his strange talent to their effort.

All of them except for Howard.

When he saw the invitations, he yelled so much about being forced to perform against his will that he made Ida burst into tears. Which made Jenna threaten to sic the Gerbellion on him.

He had retreated to his room, locked and electrified his door, and refused to come out except at mealtimes.

The rest of them continued their preparations without him, but Blue made a point of kicking Howard's door every time he walked by. Just to let him know what he thought of his behavior.

As for the Wilsons, not much had changed. Tumble's mother was still repairing everything she could get her hands on, though she had finally agreed to hire roofers to fix the leaks. Her father had finished his coconut-shampoo jingle and started working on a new one for a company that made road flares.

The Wilsons had always carried road flares in their

RV in case they drove up on a car that had broken down, but the samples the company sent them were spectacular. They were nearly as long as Tumble's arm, and when her father lit one to see how it worked, it burned for more than half an hour. The flame was guaranteed not to go out even in the heaviest of rainstorms.

Tumble added one to her emergency backpack. She thought Maximal Star would definitely approve.

Jenna trained the Gerbellion.

Ida trained herself not to fear gerbils.

Blue called his father and got no answer.

Tumble slept in the RV every night, and every morning she sneaked back into the house.

Her mother opened the mailbox one day to find a letter in a star-studded silver envelope. She put it on Tumble's bed. Then, after a moment's thought, she picked it back up.

Silver stars winked up out of the Wilsons' trash can.

And the moon, passing out of its crescent phase and growing fuller, gazed down on the heart of the swamp. Waiting.

TWENTY-SIX

A KNACK
FOR TROUBLE

Tumble perched on one of the low posts of Goat Flat's dock, and watched her mother tinker with the jon boat motor. It had taken three hours and a lot of muttering, but she seemed to think the motor would work.

Goat had hovered over the whole process, thanking Tumble and her mother every few minutes, while Millie asked Tumble not-very-subtle questions about Howard.

When Tumble mentioned that Howard was going to defeat Millie's father in a swamp cake–eating contest, she clapped her hands together and spun in a happy circle.

"Oh, Daddy will be so excited!" she said. "He's always said you can judge a person's quality by their appetite."

"Well," Tumble said dubiously, "I guess that makes Howard really high quality. You should come by and help us all with the gerbils. He'll be there."

Tumble figured setting Millie up with Howard might

be worth one half of an x. It wasn't terribly heroic, but she was so close to her goal that she couldn't afford to be picky about the projects she took on.

"Lily, focus," her mother said. "What's this piece called again?"

Tumble stared at the whatchamacallit. She didn't care much about motors, but they had been playing this game all afternoon, and it seemed to please her mother.

"The chokey?"

"Close. The choke. And what does it do?"

"You have to pull it out to start the engine," said Tumble. She slapped at a mosquito that had just bitten her arm.

"When it's cold," her mother said.

"Right," said Tumble. "When the engine's cold you have to choke it."

Her mother had started to complain about how much time she spent over at the Montgomerys', so when she'd invited Tumble to come with her today, it had seemed best to go along.

And except for the mosquitoes and the fact that the back of her neck was sunburned, it had been okay. There wasn't much planning left to do for Operation Gerbellion, anyway. It was scheduled for the next day, with everything already arranged.

Besides, Goat was so glad they'd come.

"This is wonderful!" he said breathlessly. "Just wonderful, Mrs. Wilson!"

Tumble and her mother exchanged glances and tried not to laugh.

Goat sounded like someone who was watching a baby being born instead of someone who was having his favorite fishing boat repaired. He had taken Tumble down to the sandbar earlier and shown her the aluminum canoe that he had been using to catch fish ever since his motor quit.

"It's tippy," he'd said. "You don't want to take a dip in the Okefenokee. Dangerous stuff. No thank you, ma'am."

He had looked sadly at the narrow, silvery boat. "And sometimes my old ticker just doesn't want to do so much paddling."

He'd also shown Tumble his chest freezer, which was filled with fish and swamp cakes. Goat said any Flat that didn't love swamp cakes deserved to be disowned.

He gave her a pint bag full of frozen blueberries to eat while her mother lectured about chokes and propellers.

"And what's this?" her mother asked again, pointing to a more mysterious part of the outboard.

Uh-oh. Tumble decided that the best course of action was to change the subject. "How do you know so much about boats anyway? They can't be much like RVs."

"Very different. But a motor is a motor, and I'm happy to get my hands on it."

Just like she was happy to get her hands on plugs and light fixtures and soggy-rotten carpet.

"But how did you learn it all?"

"We've all got our own thing, I guess," her mother said, sitting back on the dock and reaching up with a dirty hand to take the last blueberry from Tumble. "Grandpa Laffy is good at running his business. Your aunt Susan had such a wonderful talent for singing. I've always had a knack for repair work."

Tumble gasped and fell off the post.

"Lily!" Her mother was on her feet in a blink.

"I'm okay!" said Tumble, scrambling upright before Millie or Goat could try to help. Her teeth hurt from cracking together when she hit the dock. "Just lost my balance, you guys! Nothing weird!"

Her mother grabbed her chin and peeled her eyelids back as if invisible brain injuries might speak to her from inside of Tumble's eyeballs.

"I'm good," said Tumble. "Seriously."

She felt bright with understanding. Her mother *fixed things*. Tumble couldn't believe she'd missed it. And if LaFayettes still had talents, that meant Blue was right. Tumble wasn't fate free after all.

But Blue thought her gift was heroism, and Tumble . . . wasn't sure. Fixing things was *easy* for her mother. As much as she wished it were different, being a good hero was tough for Tumble.

"Lily, are you sure you're fine?"

"Mom, what's my knack?"

"What, sweetie?" Her mother was doing that cheek-stroking thing she always did when Tumble was hurt.

"You've got a knack for fixing things," said Tumble, stepping back. "What have I got a knack for?"

Her mother laughed. "Getting into trouble obviously! My little damsel in distress." She said it fondly. "You're going to have a bruise on your chin after that fall."

Getting into trouble.

It was like her mother had hit a switch. All of the brightness left Tumble in an instant. The bleachers. The shoplifter. Almost falling out of the Montgomerys' pecan tree. Jason.

Jason.

Tumble reached into her pocket to wrap her fingers around the plastic bag. "That can't be it," she said, shaking her head. "Mom, that can't be my knack."

Her mother smiled. "Of course not, sweetheart. I was only teasing. You're so smart. You're good at so many things."

Damsel. In. Distress.

The words settled in Tumble's gut.

And unlike Blue's assurances that she was a hero, they had the feel of rock solid truth.

TWENTY-SEVEN

MUNCHGOMERY

"You've reached Alan Montgomery! Please leave a message. He'll get back to you almost as fast as he drives."

Blue didn't leave a message.

Sometimes the unanswered calls made him feel hot all over, like someone had poured him full of gasoline and lit a match. Today, he couldn't find that feeling. He couldn't find much of anything on the inside except for a sick heaviness.

He trudged back upstairs, trying to think of things that made him angry. He wanted that heat to burn away the worry. Even the lime-green paint spilled on the banisters wasn't enough to make him mad. He tripped over one of Chet's cowboy boots, but it was hard to be angry with a three-year-old. He caught a whiff of the smelly cousin's stench on the second floor, and tried to work himself up over that.

But Blue couldn't hate someone for something they couldn't help.

Out of habit, he stopped to give Howard's door its usual kick.

Everyone knew that Ma Myrtle wanted to see Bagget Flat beaten at eating his own swamp cakes. Howard actually had a talent that could help them out, and instead of using it, he was being selfish.

The little smiley face painted on Howard's electrified doorknob grinned. Annoyance sparked inside of Blue. He kicked the door again.

Selfishness, he thought. *That's it. Howard won't share his room. He won't do his part to impress Ma Myrtle.*

He kicked the door harder. A stinging ache radiated out from the stitched-up gash on his shin. That did it.

Here Blue was, fighting so hard against his fate that he had thirty-nine stitches running up his leg. And Howard was hiding out in his own private room because he was too stuck-up to eat a few stupid pancakes.

Blue switched to his good leg and gave the door a solid kick that made his bones shake. The door rattled in its frame.

"Hey!" Howard shouted from inside the room. "Stop it!"

Blue kicked again. His foot was going to be bruised. And it was all Howard's fault.

"Don't make me come out there, Blue!" Howard shouted. "I'm not kidding."

Blue kicked one more time.

Crack.

There was a splintering sound. Blue couldn't see the damage, but he knew the sound meant he was winning. He was breaking down Howard's door.

Howard shouted something Blue couldn't hear over the fire that had suddenly roared to life inside of him. The fire wanted him to do it. It wanted him to turn Howard's door into kindling.

He backed up all the way to the wall opposite Howard's room. It was going to be like in the movies. He was going to throw his whole body at the door and explode into the room in a shower of wood chips. He lunged forward.

Just as a furious Howard yanked the door open.

Blue smashed into his cousin instead of the door and the two of them flew backward into the room.

Blue leaped up, ready to defend himself from Howard's wrath, but Howard was scrambling across the floor to slam the door shut behind them. And he didn't look angry. He looked panicked.

He jerked the bolt and reached for a tangle of wires that Blue guessed were his electrocution system. Then he leaned back against the door, closed his eyes, and took a deep breath.

"What's the matter with you?" Blue demanded. His eyes were taking in the rest of Howard's bedroom. It was full of stuff that didn't make sense.

There was a barbell in one corner and an old television in the other. It had Insane Pain Fitness discs stacked on top of it. The box of MoonPies Millie Flat had sent over weeks ago was beside them, unopened. And against the opposite wall, a jumbo-size trash bag bulged with garbage. It was so stuffed that the white plastic had stretched thin, and the contents were almost visible.

Blue could identify the previous night's sweet potato

soufflé by its orange color. And there was a stick of beef jerky poking out of the top of the bag. "What is all of this?"

Howard groaned and slid down the door to sit at the base of it with his face in his hands.

Blue realized then that he was wearing workout clothes. And he was sweaty. "Why would you work out?" he asked. "I mean . . . your whole talent is staying healthy no matter what you eat."

"I just really like to exercise," Howard said into his hands.

Blue frowned. "You like to do workouts called Insane Pain?"

Howard nodded.

"But it's some kind of a secret?" Blue's brain couldn't wrap itself around the problem. Why had Howard hidden sweet potatoes in his room? Had he just taken a plate up and then realized he didn't want to eat it?

And . . . Blue sniffed. Why was Howard keeping garbage up here when it smelled like it should have been thrown away days ago?

"Don't tell the others," Howard said. "Please. You can't."

"Well, I mean, it's weird that you would lift weights if you don't need to," said Blue. "But I don't see why the others would care."

"Because," said Howard, finally looking up. "Blue, I . . . I lied about it."

"About the weight lifting?"

"Nooo," Howard moaned. "About my talent."

"Every couple of generations, someone gets eaten," said Howard, aiming a can full of Glorious Gardenia air freshener at the garbage bag. "By the alligator. By Munch."

Blue, who had been flipping through the stack of exercise videos, looked up. "What?"

"I said *someone gets eaten by the alligator!*" Howard hissed.

"That's ridiculous," said Blue. "I've never heard of that."

"Because your dad is *so* interested in the rest of us," Howard said sarcastically. "I'm sure he tells you family stories all the time."

Blue didn't know what to say.

Howard tossed the air freshener onto his bed. "It's true," he said. "Someone will be born with a weird birthmark, shaped like an alligator tooth, or there will be something else about them . . . and then one day they'll just be gone."

"You're not going to be eaten by an alligator, Howard," said Blue. "Those other Montgomerys probably ran away from Murky Branch. People do it all the time in this family."

Howard glared. "I *know* what I'm talking about. And it's not *an* alligator. It's *the* alligator. The one from the story."

He stalked over to the window and pulled up the blinds.

"So you have a weird birthmark somewhere?" Blue said skeptically.

Howard turned the window latch. Blue noticed that there was a small decoration on the wall right beside Howard's window—Walcott Montgomery by himself, staring up at a circle. The carvings must be all over the house.

"Not a birthmark," said Howard. "In my case it was my birth certificate."

"Your birth certificate said you were going to be swallowed by a golden alligator named Munch?"

Howard lifted the window and started fanning the flowery garbage smell outside. "Sort of," he said. "When I was born, the nurse got my name wrong. Howard *Munch*gomery. That was when everyone knew."

Blue tried not to roll his eyes. "Howard . . . a typo doesn't mean you're going to be eaten."

"It's not something I just made up." Howard's voice was tight. "They say that Cousin Norabelle went all the way to Australia, hoping to avoid Munch, and she had to come back to Murky Branch for *just one night* to be a bridesmaid at her sister's wedding, and when they went to wake her up the next morning . . ."

"They saw the gator?"

"They found mud and claw marks all over the room, and the only thing left of Norabelle was a crinoline."

Blue hoped a crinoline was something like an appendix— not absolutely necessary for your continued good health.

"Maybe Norabelle was playing a joke on the family." Blue stacked the Insane Pain videos back on top of the television. "Maybe she hated her sister and wanted to give her nightmares."

Howard shook his head. "Everyone knows it happens

sometimes. Someone will be born without any apparent talent or curse, and then one day? *Gulp.*"

"Is that why your mom . . ." Blue didn't know of a nice way to put it.

"Oh, she didn't want one of us messed-up Montgomery kids," Howard said bitterly, slamming the window back down. "She was hoping for some bright little starlet, just like herself. Granny Eve won't even talk to her."

"But if everyone knew you were going to be . . . munched on . . . when you were born, then why—"

Howard stared out the window. "It was always so depressing, you know? Even when I was a little kid. People would look at me, and they would get sad. Then, when I was six or so, Granny Eve made these miniature strawberry cupcakes for the twins' birthday. I started shoving them into my mouth as fast as I could, and I think it was Jenna who said, 'Wow, he really is a Munchgomery!'"

He pressed his forehead to the glass.

"I just thought how nice it would be if she was right. If I were one of the lucky ones. So, I started to eat tons of food any time anyone was watching me, and then they all got kind of hopeful. Pretty soon I was stuffing my face all the time, and they finally decided that it could be a talent. Like, maybe I was this eating machine, who could just eat whatever, whenever, without any consequences."

"So you pretended it was true?" said Blue.

"Well, you know, for a while I thought it might be. I wanted it to be. But then I ate four bowls of Frosted Flakes one morning, and it made me barf. Only by then . . . I couldn't tell anyone the truth."

"Because they'd stop looking at you like you were someone special," Blue said.

"Yeah." Howard turned back around. "I wanted to be one of the special ones. But it was more than that. I don't want them all to worry about me."

Blue couldn't imagine fooling people for that long. "So you work out a lot."

"Sure," said Howard, flexing his arms so that his muscles stood out. "I *do* enjoy it, but it also deflects suspicion. I try to eat a lot of protein and vegetables. And I have all of these tricks—I hid eight pieces of French toast under my shirt once without anyone noticing."

"Gross."

"Yeah. And it's wasteful," said Howard. "But if it keeps people from knowing the truth, I'm okay with that. Granny Eve doesn't need to be afraid for me on top of everything else."

"Howard," said Blue, suddenly remembering. "The swamp cake–eating contest—"

"I'm doomed," Howard groaned. "But I guess I always was."

TWENTY-EIGHT

THE ONLY
DIFFERENCE

"It'll be fine," Blue promised Howard. "Everything's going to be great with the gerbils tomorrow. Ma Myrtle will be so impressed there won't even *be* a Grand Revue. You won't have to eat a million swamp cakes without puking."

The two of them had been talking for over an hour, and it was almost time for supper. Blue would be watching closely to see what his cousin did with his meal.

"Are you even a member of this family?" Howard said, fiddling with the battery pack and wires that powered his electric-shock system. "It's *never* that easy."

"It will be," said Blue. "It's going to work great. We've got it all planned out."

"Six seconds," said Howard.

"What?"

Howard pointed toward an empty plate on the floor

beside his dresser. It was covered in green crumbs and cane syrup. "I've been practicing. I *hate* the Flats' pancakes. They taste like green dye, and they stick to the roof of your mouth. But I can eat one every six seconds."

"Maybe that will be—"

"I've seen Bagget Flat eat," said Howard. "He can probably do three times that many."

They both fell silent, contemplating the empty plate.

"I guess we should go," Howard said after a moment. "Do me a favor and take those MoonPies with you. I told Millie I liked them once so that she would stop bringing me swamp cakes. But I'm kind of sick of everything with the word *moon* on it."

Blue fetched the box, and by the time he turned around, Howard was unwrapping the final wire from the doorknob.

"Why'd you burst in here anyway?" he asked before he turned it. "What did I do to make you so mad?"

Blue didn't say anything.

Howard gave him a long look. "Or were you mad at somebody else?"

"I'm sorry about kicking your door."

Howard still hadn't turned the knob. "You know," he said, "your dad leaving you here isn't your fault."

Blue looked down at the box in his hands. The yellow crescent moon on the top of it was smirking up at him. "Yeah."

"Listen," said Howard. "Ida's always telling me to keep my thoughts to myself. She's all, 'Let Blue figure this out on his own, Howard.' And, 'You don't know what Uncle Alan might be dealing with, Howard.'"

Blue's head jerked up. "You've talked about me behind my back?"

"A little. Anyway, I just wanted to make sure you know it's not even *about* you. Your dad leaving you . . . it's about him."

Blue forced a smile onto his face. "Okay. Fine. Great. Can we go to supper now?"

Howard frowned. "Yeah, okay. Just remember what I said."

"Got it."

"And Granny Eve's not mad about you being here, either. In case you were worried. She's just mad that your dad wants to race again. After the last time, with his talent causing all those wrecks . . ." Howard opened the door. "She's afraid he's going to get someone killed."

Howard stepped out into the hall, but Blue was too dumbstruck to follow him.

"Hey," said Howard, looking around, "don't leave me standing here with the door open. Someone might see my—"

"What?"

"I said don't leave me stand—"

"No." Blue took a step toward him. "What do you mean, he caused the wrecks? Those were accidents."

Howard raised an eyebrow at him. "What do you think happens when your dad *isn't* the best racer on the track?"

"He's always the best racer on the track."

"No," said Howard. "He always *wins*. It's not the same thing at all."

"That's not—"

"Blue," Howard interrupted. He pointed to the stitches running up Blue's shin. "The only difference between you and your dad, is that when your dad races, it's everyone else who gets tackled by the deer."

TWENTY-NINE

JUST ONE GERBIL
AT A TIME

"**I** think," said Tumble, "that somebody ought to find that alligator and give it a kick in the tail, before it ruins anyone else's life."

It was the next morning, and the two of them were sprawled across the beanbag chair in the attic. They were eating Howard's MoonPies and watching the dust motes swirl over their heads. Blue had just told Tumble about what his cousin had said.

He had stayed up all night, trying hard not to believe it, but the more he tried, the more questions he had. How *did* his dad win everything? He wasn't the strongest man in the world, and he was fast but not the fastest.

In fact, Blue's dad was pretty normal.

But his talent let him win. Every single time.

How?

By making everyone else lose. It had to be the truth.

Only, Blue had never known the truth was something that could gnaw on you with invisible teeth.

"Maybe if you got your dad's side of the story . . ." said Tumble.

"He'd have to answer the phone for that to happen."

"Ah," she said. "Right."

"What did you want to tell me again?" Blue asked. "Before I mentioned Howard and my dad and . . . all of it."

Tumble hesitated. "Nothing major."

"You said it was about your fate."

"It's not important. I mean . . . it's . . . it might not matter after today anyway. Breaking Ida's curse might get rid of the fates for good."

"I'm trying not to be too hopeful," Blue said. "If it convinces Ma Myrtle to send the relatives away and tell the twins how to find Munch, that will be enough. For today."

"You have to think more positively," said Tumble. *"Doubters can't be do-gooders."* She sat up and reached for her emergency backpack. "Here, let me show you something."

She pulled a wrinkled silver envelope out of the front pocket. It was covered in tiny sparkling stars.

"It's from the Maximal Star Young Heroes Fan Club," she said, passing it to Blue. "I found it in the trash can."

"Your parents threw it away?" said Blue, outraged. "Without telling you!"

"They don't trust me to take care of myself. They think that they're keeping me safe by bringing me out here where I can't see anyone or do anything, and I guess Maximal Star doesn't fit into their plans."

Blue pulled the flyer out of the envelope and read it. "It says Maximal Star's on tour! He's going to be in Georgia."

"I looked it up on a map," said Tumble. "The town is about an hour away from here."

"But they have to let you go." Blue waved the flyer at her. He didn't care about Maximal Star, but this would be a huge deal for Tumble. "He's your hero. And you're a hero. And this is a huge heroing event! How many chances like that do you get?"

"They don't think I can do it," said Tumble. "They never have."

"Well," said Blue, "you're going to prove them wrong today."

They didn't have much longer to wait. Ida was doing breathing exercises to relax herself before the ordeal. Howard and Jenna were preparing the Gerbellion for their most important mission ever. And Millie Flat had volunteered to help.

When it was time, Tumble pulled Blue to his feet.

"This is it," she announced to the attic at large. "Today, we're going to break a curse. And we're going to prove to everyone that there's nothing wrong with us. And everything is going to be terrific."

Ida wasn't terrific. She was terrified.

Blue had gone to fetch her while Tumble, Howard, and Millie were setting up the Gerbellion's maze in the front yard. The maze included gerbil-size tight ropes and tubing and staircases. According to Jenna, the gerbils could navigate it in under a minute on a good day.

If the exhibition was going well, Ida was supposed to help Jenna direct the gerbils through the maze to a pile of sunflower seeds. But that was advanced stuff, and Ida was in an advanced state of panic.

"I kn-know you all th-think I'm a big dumb cow-coward," she stammered. She was huddled in the corner of the twins' bedroom, shaking.

"Well . . . you're not dumb," said Jenna.

Blue glared at her.

They were both crouching beside Ida, who was crushing her hands to her head in misery.

"You're *not* a coward," he said to Ida. "It's not wrong to be afraid of things that can really hurt you."

It was Jenna's turn to glare. *Excuse me?* she mouthed at Blue. *Not helping.*

But Blue thought he knew what he was talking about better than Jenna ever could. "It's not wrong to be afraid," he insisted. "It's smart, actually. If you were dumb, you'd run around trying to pet cats, and you wouldn't wear snake boots, and you'd probably be all kinds of dead."

Ida finally looked up at him. "So why am I d-doing this?" she said. "It's c-crazy!"

"Because," said Blue, "sometimes being smart and

afraid isn't okay anymore. Sometimes being afraid of losing is worse than *actually* losing. And when it gets that bad, you've got to do something different. Even if it's a little crazy."

Ida took big, slow breaths, trying to calm down. "I could . . ." She swallowed. "I could hold . . . maybe . . . just one gerbil at a time. Like yesterday?"

Jenna hesitated. "That's not what we planned—"

"That'll be fine," said Blue.

Ida was the kind of person who gave you a lemon cake candle and a beanbag chair to welcome you to your attic. Blue wasn't sure about a lot of things lately, but he was sure that she didn't deserve to be bullied into saying yes.

THIRTY

THE STAPLER

"**B**ut, Blue!" Tumble said frantically. "This won't work! It won't break the curse, and Ma Myrtle won't be impressed. She'll want to see more."

They were standing in the front yard behind a pair of tables covered with the gerbil cages and the maze. The porch was filling with droopy-looking relatives. Competing for Ma Myrtle's favor was starting to wear on them all.

"Ma Myrtle needs to get over herself," said Blue.

"*Yes*," said Tumble, "and she won't do that if we don't knock her socks off right now!"

Blue shook his head.

"I can't believe you. We *just* talked about this—"

"Don't be mean to Ida about it, okay?" he snapped. "She's *my* cousin, and she's really scared, and I don't want you to."

Tumble made herself be silent for a few seconds, just to be sure she wasn't being unreasonable.

She wasn't.

"Blue, *so what* if Ida gets a little scared? This could change her whole *life*. It might even save your entire family!"

"It's not right."

Tumble groaned. "It's gerbils!" she said, making the itsy-bitsy gesture with two of her fingers. "They're *tiny*."

"Tumble, *just don't*," he hissed as the twins emerged from the house.

"Blue, we've been planning this for ages."

"Don't."

By the time Ma Myrtle appeared, everyone was sweating.

Tumble's hair stuck to her face and her neck, and she was sure at least half of the moisture running down her back was from nerves. Blue was wrong about this. He just was. He was looking at poor Ida, and he was feeling sorry for her, and Tumble got it.

She did.

She felt sorry for Ida, too. But you didn't let someone

make a terrible mistake just because they were frightened. You grabbed a pair of long johns and a stapler, and you kept them from going over the edge of the building.

Tumble didn't know how she was going to do that yet, but she plucked her emergency backpack off the ground and put it on as Ma Myrtle started in on a very unhelpful speech about how Ida would probably "perish in the attempt."

The fourth Tenet of Heroism was *ever-prepared*. The backpack was heavy, and it was hot. But Tumble had a solution in it for every occasion, and she wasn't about to be caught offguard.

While Ma Myrtle rambled, she ran through a mental list of her supplies and tried to find a use for them all. Water bottle in case of dehydration. Bug spray because bug spray was important when you lived near a swamp. First aid kit for bites, cuts, and abrasions. Pocketknife for cutting bandages. Heimlich-maneuver sheet . . . in case someone choked on a gerbil? Waterproof matches, diaper pins, roadside flare, trail mix—Tumble didn't know how any of that was going to be useful, but she would figure it out if a problem arose.

By the time she'd finished her inventory, Ma Myrtle had finished talking. It was time.

If this went right, really right, Tumble could cross off the last *x*'s. She could be different. She would know that she was a hero and not a damsel. Other people didn't have to save her. It would be over. She reached a hand into her pocket and her fingers found her brother's picture. *Just a few more minutes.*

Ida stood by the table, swaying on her feet.

Jenna reached into the first cage and carefully lifted the friendliest gerbil out.

Ida raised her cupped hands in front of her, staring straight ahead like she was about to walk a gangplank, and Jenna set the pale brown gerbil on her palms.

The people on the porch drew in a collective breath and held it, waiting for the inevitable. The gerbil would bite Ida's fingers. Or it would claw its way up her bare arms and go for her throat.

No one was expecting a fatal wound from such a small animal, but they were expecting something more than what they got.

Which was nothing.

Jenna was leaning over the gerbil, whispering "Don't bite, don't bite," and the gerbil was quivering with suppressed loathing, and then . . . it was over. Jenna lifted the gerbil out of her twin's hands and passed it to Howard, who had been tasked with putting it back in its pen.

Millie Flat, who was in charge of preventing an en masse gerbil escape, slid the top screen open for him and then snapped it back into place without ever glancing at Howard's face.

The experiment was repeated again. And again.

It wasn't working. Tumble could tell. There was no sign of Ida's curse fading; the gerbils obviously still hated her. The third one even held its open mouth against her finger for a breathtaking second.

But Jenna was able to soothe them all. This plan wasn't messing up her talent even a little. The Montgomery fates were just too strong.

By the third gerbil, Ma Myrtle was looking pretty soothed herself. Tumble had been right. They weren't going to convince Blue's great-grandmother to call off the Revue this way or tell the twins how to find Munch or . . . anything useful.

Ida wasn't letting it go far enough. They needed to do something bigger. Even if they didn't make it to the maze, they had to go back to the basic plan at least.

Ida was supposed to hold all nine of the gerbils at once.

Tumble took a deep breath. Blue would be mad, but not for long. Not after Ida discovered that she didn't have to be afraid of animals anymore. Not after Tumble proved that their fates didn't have to be set in stone.

The failure to act in the face of danger is a failure you can't afford.

There was danger here, real and true, even if Blue couldn't see it clearly.

Tumble took a step toward the gerbil cages.

"Excuse me," Howard said loudly, crossing his arms over his chest. "What do you think you're doing?"

Tumble froze, one hand on top of the screen that separated the used gerbils from the outside world. She had expected Howard to notice her, of course. Even if

Millie was too busy staring at her feet to know what was going on with everyone else, Howard was standing right by the cages, too.

But Tumble had thought he would ask her quietly what was going on, so as not to interrupt the twins.

And she would say she just wanted to hold one of the gerbils.

And Howard would say something like *okay, as long as you're careful.*

And then Tumble would, in fact, be careful. She would be very careful as she carried the friendliest little gerbil over and set it ever so gently on top of Ida's rainbow hair.

Jenna would do her whispering thing, and Ida would be scared. But only at first! She would get more confident as time passed and she held two gerbils, and neither of them tried to murder her. And then the show could go on the way it was *supposed* to.

Everyone would see that Tumble really had done it. She had figured out how to beat fate.

But for some reason, Howard was *loud.* And every eye turned to stare at Tumble.

"What are you doing?" said Blue.

Tumble didn't know. She couldn't go through with the original plan, not with everyone on the alert.

And she couldn't admit defeat.

Not today.

Blue must have seen the determination settle over her face. He reached for her. "Tumble! Don't!"

Tumble jerked the screen off the pen, and five gerbils hopped out and turned their beady black eyes toward Ida.

"Everybody hold still!" Howard commanded, holding his hands out to either side to fend off anyone who might be thinking of coming near the freed gerbils. "Don't startle them!"

"Ida, don't move!" Jenna cried. "Don't bite! Don't bite!"

For three seconds, it was fine.

Then Ida cracked.

She thrust the gerbil in her hands at Jenna so forcefully that her sister fell back into the grass, and she took off running through the yard, sobbing with terror.

The Gerbellion leaped for the ground.

Millie and Howard dove to intercept, and Tumble

watched with horror as a gerbil landed right on top of Howard's head. It was the gerbil Millie had been trying to catch, and she was moving so fast that she couldn't stop, and—

Tumble winced as Millie's fist connected with Howard's nose.

The people on the porch were dashing here and there and knocking one another into the shrubs. Some of them were screaming about mice even though the gerbils were nowhere near them.

Blue had already dashed after Ida.

"I'm sorry!" Tumble cried. But nobody was paying any attention.

Jenna was cradling the gerbil in her hands, checking it for injuries even as it struggled, eager to join the hunt for her sister. Millie was on the ground, clutching a gerbil and staring woefully up at Howard while he tried to use the hem of his shirt to stop the flow of blood from his nose.

And Ida . . .

Tumble looked around in time to see her throwing herself into Greg Montgomery's fireproof tent.

Blue was hot on her heels. No doubt the gerbils were, too.

Tumble had to help. She had to undo the damage.

She ran for the tent, her backpack bouncing behind her. By the time she reached it, Blue had climbed into the little two-man tent as well. It now had three Montgomerys in it, and possibly a pack of bloodthirsty rodents.

The dark yellow fabric was writhing and bulging in odd places. Tumble could hear Greg's confused shouts, and Ida's terrified wails, and Blue saying, "Where are they? Do you see them!?"

The tent fabric ripped, and Greg's arm appeared, waving crazily.

Tumble wasn't sure if it was an accident or if the fire starter was trying to escape. "I'm here!" she said as she ran toward the arm. "Can I help? Where are the gerbils?"

She saw movement in the grass and bent over to see if she could spot a flash of fur. But it was only a lizard, skittering sideways into the fray as if compelled against its better judgment. As Tumble sraightened, Greg's flailing hand slapped her backpack.

Tumble heard a loud hiss.

Snakes! That was her first thought. Snakes must be coming for Ida, too.

The situation couldn't get any worse.

The tent gave up and ripped all the way. Ida, Greg, Blue, four gerbils, and at least two lizards sprawled across the grass. Blue had a gerbil clutched in each hand. Greg had one as well. And the fourth was crawling up the front of Ida's shirt.

"You got them!" Tumble said, relieved.

Then Greg dropped his gerbil on the ground, pointed at Tumble, and screamed "FIRE!"

The hissing, thought Tumble. *And Greg's hand hitting my backpack. And . . .*

The road flare. Tumble's pulse surged. She started fighting to get the straps off her shoulders. Something was stuck; she was stuck!

The heat. She could feel it. Her emergency pack was supposed to be flame retardant, but a road flare was something else. She was going to—

Greg had one of his fire extinguishers in his hands

so quickly it looked like he had conjured it. He blasted Tumble's backpack furiously, with the air of someone who had done it many times before, and she stumbled forward.

But that wouldn't work.

"It's a flare!" she screamed. "It's a flare!"

Greg gaped at her in horror.

Blue seemed confused about how to help when he had his hands filled with gerbils.

Then Ida was there, ripping Tumble's arms through the backpack's straps, freeing her just as the hissing, burning light tore through the back of the bag.

Ida threw it away from herself onto the ground. "Don't let it catch the grass on fire!"

Greg started spraying the backpack with the extinguisher again.

"Thank you," Tumble said in a small voice.

The whole fiasco had taken seconds. Blue's grandmother was running across the yard toward them, a sloshing pitcher full of tea in her hand. Most of the liquid was gone by the time she reached them, but she dumped the last of it on top of the still-burning bag anyway.

"Oh, sweet mercy," Eve said, tossing the pitcher aside and rounding to face Tumble. In a moment, she was spinning her in circles, checking her all over for injuries.

Tumble didn't think she was hurt. At least not that way.

"It's a miracle," said Eve. "That's what! Girl, what were you thinking, carrying a flare in your backpack?! Of all the foolish—"

"Owww," Ida said.

Tumble looked around. A gerbil had attached itself to Ida's earlobe. Blue was biting his lower lip as he tried to pry the little creature off without dropping the two in his hands.

"I can—" said Tumble.

"No, you can't," said Blue. He finally managed to coax the gerbil's jaws open.

Ida reached up to touch her bleeding ear.

"You let the gerbils out," said Blue, turning back to look at Tumble like he'd never seen her before.

"I was just trying to help."

"No, you weren't!" Ida shouted. "You were just trying to get what you wanted! I don't want you coming back over here!"

"Ida, honey," said Eve.

"I'm sorry," said Tumble, aghast. "I'm really—"

"Not as sorry as I am," said Ida, tears welling up in her eyes as she fell against her grandmother's chest. There was blood trickling down her neck. "Go away! You *ruined* it. I was doing it. It was g-going okay. You only m-made it all turn out *bad*."

Tumble looked at the Montgomerys spread across the yard. A few of them were still running around in a panic. Others were hobbling along with scraped knees and elbows from being shoved off the porch. Jenna was combing the grass, searching for any signs of her pets. Even Ma Myrtle had collapsed onto the swing, looking genuinely upset for the first time since Tumble had met her.

And Millie was sitting where she'd fallen, her whole body gone limp as a rag doll's. She was staring longingly at Howard's bloody face.

"I didn't mean for it to go wrong," Tumble said, turning back to face Blue. She took a step toward him. "I
only wanted to help."

"I told you not to mess with Ida," Blue said.

"Blue, I *needed* to help her." Tumble wished now that
she had told him what she suspected. If Blue had known
that she was worried about being a damsel in distress, he
would have understood.

But he didn't know. He looked away.

"*I* think you should leave, too."

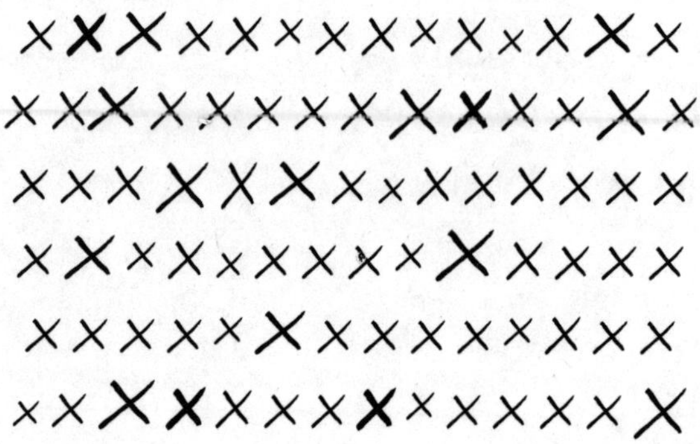

THIRTY-ONE

ULTIMATUM

Blue hadn't realized how much he depended on Tumble's company until he didn't have it anymore. In the days that followed the attack of the Gerbellion, he was alone with his thoughts. He agonized over words. Words he'd said to Tumble. Words Howard had said to him. Words his dad had never said.

When your dad races, it's everyone else who gets tackled by the deer.

Why hadn't Blue ever wondered? People *died* in car crashes.

One night, he couldn't stand it anymore.

A few hours before dawn he put on his running shoes, tucked his cell phone into the back pocket of his shorts, and crept downstairs. He slipped past Cousin Ernestine, who was sleeping on the sofa with her mouth hanging wide open, and headed for the front door.

Blue ran through the darkness, harder and faster and farther than he ever had before.

The sky was blacker than it had been on the first night he'd arrived in Murky Branch. He had trouble seeing the ground in front of him. But he didn't fall. He ran past the sign, not looking at the number on it, reaching into his pocket automatically to stop his cell phone's timer.

He ran to the paved road.

He ran, as fast as he could, away from Murky Branch.

Toward the end, he had to pause several times to breathe, and once, he had to duck out of sight before a passing car could spot him. But Blue made it. He crossed over whatever invisible line separated Murky Branch from the rest of the world.

He stopped and looked around at the empty road, the tall pines, the metal mile marker standing like a sentinel not far away. No one would be eavesdropping on him out here.

Blue found a place to sit on the side of the road, with his back resting against the rough bark of a pine tree. The ground beneath him was cushioned with fallen pine straw, and the muggy night air was cool against his over-heated skin.

His legs were shaky. His hands were, too, but that was different.

Blue pulled out his phone.

The stopped timer was the first thing he saw when the screen lit. Thirteen minutes, nine seconds. It was his best time yet.

He didn't know if that mattered anymore.

He dialed the number slowly. He wouldn't leave a message this time. His questions were too big for messages. Blue was going to make the phone ring and ring and ring until his dad had no choice but to pick up.

And when he did, Blue would be calm. He wouldn't accuse his dad of anything. He wouldn't whine. He would just ask.

It took four calls.

"Hi there, Skeeter," his dad said in a tired voice. "Everything okay down there?"

"When you win . . . do other people get hurt?"

The silence was a chasm between them.

Blue waited and waited. Finally, he said, "I want you to come back to Murky Branch. Come and stay here. With me."

"Did your Granny tell you that?" his dad asked, voice tight.

"You need to come back."

His dad inhaled sharply. "Now listen here, Blue. What I do for my job is my own business. And your granny is overreacting if she's filling your head with that mess. People get hurt all the time. Not every little thing is our fault."

Blue was on his feet. He didn't remember standing up. "Why can't you have some other job? Why do you have to win?"

"I just said that's not for you to worry about. I'll pick you up at the end of the summer, just like I promised. Isn't that what you want?"

Blue squeezed his eyes shut. "No."

"What?"

"No!" the word felt awful in his mouth. And true. "I don't want you to pick me up at the end of the summer. I want you to come back right now. I want you to quit racing, and I want you to stay here with me, and I want you never to win again."

"Well, Skeeter, that's not the plan," his dad said flippantly. "You don't understand—"

He doesn't think I'm serious.

"I understand better than you ever will!" Blue shouted. "You don't *have* to compete. You just like it. And it's not fair to anyone else, and you know you're doing something wrong, and that's why you left me here, *isn't it?*"

"That's not . . . it's not true." For the first time, his dad sounded uncertain. "I gave you some bad advice about that boy at school. I know that. I didn't mean for you to be hurt. Once I have my next steps all figured out, I'll come back for you. It'll be like before."

That was when Blue knew. His dad didn't get it. Maybe he didn't want to get it. He wanted this to be about a fistfight and a broken arm.

That wasn't what it was about at all.

"It *can't* be like before," Blue tried to explain. "You can't be a racer. You can't keep making other people lose."

Now that Blue knew, he wouldn't be able to stand it.

"Well, what *can* I be if you're making all the rules?"

He was mad. Of course he was mad. Blue leaned against the tree for support.

"You can be my dad," he said. "You can be someone who . . . does the right thing."

"I don't know where the heck you're getting this idea that I'm some horrible person!"

"You don't know what it's like," said Blue. "You don't know what it's like to lose."

"This conversation is over," his dad said. "Don't call again unless you feel like apologizing. I'll be back for you at the end of the summer. We'll talk about it then."

Blue took a deep breath. "If you're not going to give up racing and come for me right now," he said, "then I think you shouldn't bother coming back at all."

THIRTY-TWO

NO PLACE
FOR WINNERS

I t was over. It was done. Blue's dad *wasn't* going to
change for him, and he wasn't going to come for him.

When he finally passed the Murky Branch sign again,
Blue didn't remind it that he wasn't planning on staying.
He just thought of his thirteen minutes and his nine
seconds and wondered how the walk back to his grandmother's house could feel so much longer.

You shouldn't bother coming back at all, he'd said.

He couldn't believe he'd said that. He couldn't believe
he'd meant it.

He saw the Wilsons' RV as he stumbled past their
house, and he wanted with an aching kind of want to
go up to the door and knock. He knew Tumble would
be in there.

But he'd told her to go away.

Blue watched his borrowed shoes fall one in front of

the other all the way back to the Montgomery house.

He had to do something to fight back against this horrible shredding inside of him. He needed someone to talk to. Or something to break.

But when he made it to the house, nobody was awake. And nothing in this place was his to break.

The only thing he could do was escape to his attic. Because it *was* his now. *And maybe . . .*

He tried to stop the thought but couldn't. Not this time. Maybe this had *always* been permanent, and he hadn't been able to let himself realize it.

He reached up to pull the chain on the light and looked around. There was nothing in here that was his own except for his clothes. Not the air mattress. Not the poster. And not, *not ever*, the boxes.

He went to the nearest one and opened it. Gold gleamed up at him from the pointed tip of a trophy with a ballerina on top.

Blue bent to pick it up. He tried to read the name on the bottom, but it was in elegant cursive, and he wasn't seeing right. Something was blurring his vision.

It doesn't matter, Blue thought. *No one cares about the ballerina. They left her in the attic.*

He shoved the box closer to the window. The trophies inside—all of those forgotten victories—rattled and clinked as if they knew what Blue was going to do.

He fumbled with the latch on the window and forced it open. Granny Eve's huge garden was below him in the half-light of approaching dawn. Blue looked down.

Some of us don't get to stand in spotlights on stages, he thought, gripping the ballerina so that the edges of her plastic tutu cut into his fingers. *Some of us don't get anything but dirt.*

He threw her away from him, as far as he could. She twinkled as she plunged toward the ground, but Blue didn't see. He was already bending over, ripping at the nearest box. Medals and ribbons, trophies and tiaras—he didn't care what or whose or why. He would get rid of them all.

The attic was his now.

And it wasn't a place for winners.

THIRTY-THREE

THE
DAMSEL

Tumble hadn't seen Blue in almost three days.

She lay facedown on Mr. Patty's dusty-smelling sofa and listened to the stomping and banging coming from overhead. The roofers had finally come to patch the leaks.

She breathed in more dust, and covered the back of her head with her arms to drown out the sound. Lying here, it had occurred to her that you did not pay to fix the roof of a house you were only renting for a few months. You didn't start talking about hardwood floors and new light fixtures if you were planning on leaving in just a little while.

Tumble didn't know why she had never realized that every broken thing her mother repaired was one more sign they would be in Murky Branch for a long, long time. She was starting to wonder if they had actually *bought* the house from Mr. Patty, and they hadn't wanted to tell her in case her poor fragile brain couldn't handle it.

And obviously her brain *couldn't* handle it, because if they told her they were moving here for good, Tumble thought she would scream and scream. And if they ever tried to get rid of the RV, she thought she would die.

I don't even have a friend here. Not anymore.

She had reread *How to Hero Every Day* again, but there was nothing at all on how to make your friends not hate you when your heroing efforts were a disaster. It was like Maximal Star had never made a mistake in his whole career.

Which was more proof that Tumble was cursed. She tried to think back, on every good thing she'd done and every *x* she'd gotten rid of. Even though she'd helped people, she'd always, always managed to put herself in danger doing it.

Someone else had had to rescue her. Every single time.

She didn't have any hope of getting rid of the marks against her. Especially not now that she had had to add *x*'s for Ida and Howard and the Gerbellion and Millie and on and on. . . .

If she tried again, she would only mess up, and make more mistakes she couldn't erase.

She felt the sofa dip at her feet. Someone had sat down. She clenched her arms tighter over her head. Maybe whichever parent it was would decide she wasn't worth the trouble.

Her mother's voice said, "Is it really so terrible here?"

The strange thing was, it hadn't been. The house, of course, was a ruin. And the weather was too hot and sticky. But it had been okay. Tumble had found Blue.

Of course, that was before Tumble knew that her parents meant for this to be a long-term arrangement. It was before she realized that they weren't just thinking she needed a change of pace or a house without wheels. It was before she discovered that they were right to worry—there actually was something wrong with her.

She couldn't say any of that out loud, though.

Instead, she mumbled, "Blue's mad at me," into the sofa cushions. It came out so muffled that her mother couldn't possibly have heard her.

Tumble sat up. "Blue's mad at me," she said again.

Her mother frowned. "What did you do?"

Tumble hated that she just assumed Tumble had done something wrong. "What makes you think it's *my* fault! Is everything always my fault? Just because you think I can't do anything right—"

"Lily, I didn't mean it like that," her mother said, leaning back onto the sofa. She sounded tired. "I don't think everything is your fault. I meant to say, 'What happened?'"

Tumble, thought Tumble. *Tumble, Tumble, Tumble.* Maybe if her mother had ever believed in her enough to use her hero name. Maybe if she had given Tumble a little more support.

But Tumble didn't even think that herself anymore. Her parents had been right all along, hadn't they? She pulled her knees up to her chest and wrapped her arms around them. "It *was* my fault, though," she said. "His cousin Ida . . . she's really scared of animals, and we were trying to help her get over her fear."

Tumble tried to think of what to say next. Her mother didn't know about the fates, and Tumble didn't want to tell her. It would only confirm everything she thought about Tumble, and then her parents would probably keep her trapped in this house until she was older than Ma Myrtle.

"So we were training her to hold gerbils," said Tumble.

"Gerbils?" Her mother looked confused.

"Right," said Tumble, "because gerbils are small and friendly. Only Ida backed out at the last minute, and she didn't want to go along with the plan, and I kind of . . . made her do it anyway."

Tumble could get away with this watered-down version of the truth because nobody from the Montgomery house had thought to tell her parents that Tumble had released a pack of crazed rodents and almost burned herself to death with a road flare.

Tumble had thought for sure someone would call them, and she hadn't gotten any sleep that first night, waiting for the inevitable consequences. After all, you couldn't go around catching yourself on fire and expect to get away with it.

Especially not when that was how your brother . . .

Tumble shoved the thought away.

It hadn't happened. No phone call had come, no knock on the front door. And Tumble had decided that maybe the Montgomerys didn't know how normal families worked. Or maybe they did, but they were all too busy with their own problems to bother tattling on her.

"Isn't Ida a lot older than you?" her mother asked. "I'm not sure how you could make a teenager do something she didn't want to do."

"Well," said Tumble, "Blue didn't want me to do anything to scare her. But I didn't agree, and I maybe freed some of the gerbils."

"Oh, Lily." She was massaging a spot on the center of her forehead. "Why would—"

"I thought it would be fine!" said Tumble. "I thought she needed some help was all."

"'Needed some help,'" her mother said. "So it's that again."

Tumble stared at the floor. It was funny how you could have an awkward silence even with people hammering on the roof right over your head.

"I just don't understand," her mother said, "why everything has to be Maximal Star all the time. When did you decide that the whole world needed saving and you were the only one who could do it?"

She didn't sound angry. Only frustrated.

"Helping people is important, though," said Tumble.

"Of course it is," her mother said. "And when you see someone you can help, you should. I'm so proud of you for always worrying so much about others."

"Then why—"

"Some people need help, but they don't need *your* help, Lily. At least not directly. They need help from their parents or their teachers or, heaven forbid, the authorities. When you see someone robbing a 7-Eleven, you call the police, you don't dash in yourself!"

"But . . ." Tumble could feel the pencil in her pocket, the eraser, and the picture with its dozens and dozens of new *x*'s.

"You never used to worry so much about all of the world's wrongs," her mother said. "It's something your father and I talk about a lot. We came here because we think you need time to be a kid. We don't want you to be miserable. We just want you to have a safe place to grow up. We want you to have friends you don't have to leave behind every couple of months."

"That's not working out," Tumble said glumly to her kneecaps.

Her mother leaned over and wrapped her arm around Tumble's shoulders. "You know," she said, "we all mess up and hurt our friends once in awhile. The solution is the same no matter how old you are."

"I already tried apologizing," said Tumble. "Right after it happened."

"Hmm . . ." her mother said. "Sometimes apologies work better after you've given people time and space to grow."

THIRTY-FOUR

GARDENING

Trophies had speared the watermelons. They had dented the tomato cages. The corn was decorated with glittering medals, and tiaras winked at Blue from between rows of okra and butter beans.

He had been cleaning the garden up since sunrise, and he wasn't even half finished. The energy that had driven him while he was throwing everything out the attic window had left him now that he was trying to undo the damage.

"All right," said a voice behind him. "What's this about?"

Dread dragged Blue's shoulders down like a weight. He turned to see his grandmother standing there in her housedress and gardening shoes. Her hands were on her hips as she took in the sight of pierced melons and crushed leaves.

"I'm so sorry," said Blue, dropping the muddy ballerina trophy into one of the boxes he'd brought down
with him. "I didn't mean to ruin your garden. I was mad
at Dad, and I wasn't thinking, and . . ."

He waited for her to yell at him. He knew he deserved it. She worked so hard on her garden, and with
everything else going on, Blue should have been trying
to make her life easier.

Instead he'd ruined something special.

Eve stooped to pluck a track medal off a squash plant.
She turned it over in her hands and brushed a clump of
soil from the ribbon.

"Oh, Blue, what are we going to do with you?"

"Is he right?" Blue asked. "Is Howard right about my
dad?"

He and his grandmother were sitting on top of overturned plastic buckets in the middle of the wrecked garden. Blue had explained what Howard had said, and he'd
told her about the phone call. His grandmother hadn't
interrupted the whole time he spoke.

Now she rubbed her hands together and said, "Your

daddy shouldn't be out racing. He must know it deep down. He does cause more harm than he ought to, though I'm sure he doesn't mean it."

"Oh," said Blue, his voice small. He'd known, but when she said it, the last tiny hope inside of him shriveled into nothing.

"But Howard's not right about everything. At least I don't think so," his grandmother continued. "It's never easy to get inside another person's head, but I think your daddy meant to do right by you when he left you here."

"It doesn't matter," said Blue. "It's over. I told him to come back for me right away or not to come back at all."

Eve shook her head. "Why people do what they do always matters," she said. "In your daddy's case, he's finally starting to understand that he might not be able to be what you need. Bouncing around from hotel to hotel and city to city isn't how a boy is supposed to grow up."

"But I never minded that."

"And there's also the fact that Alan's been treating you like you're a copy of him, when you're your own person with your own problems."

"He wanted me to fight back. Like he would have. Only I can't be that way."

His grandmother leaned forward and patted his knee. "I think that's what he's realizing. That you two are different, and he doesn't know how to handle you. He barely knows how to handle himself."

Blue didn't see how he was hard to handle. It wasn't like he was some exotic flower that had to be pruned with care.

"Alan was awfully young when you were born, Blue. And on top of that, he's *never* had to struggle for anything in his life. With that talent of his . . . well, I've never been sure Alan got one of the good fates. It's just as much a curse to my way of thinking. If things have always come easily to you, you don't know how to deal with trouble when it finally catches up."

Blue pondered that. What if he had never lost at anything? Would he even understand how hard losing was?

"Howard said Dad was just selfish."

Eve was silent for a moment. "Blue," she said, "I don't think it's right to lie to you, but I want you to listen close. Your daddy has always loved being the best, and he's never cared enough about the people he passed by on his way to first place. That's true."

That's selfish, thought Blue.

"*But,*" said his grandmother, "nobody is all one way or the other. There is good in Alan, too. And I think when he brought you to me, he was trying to be good. He knows I don't approve of what he's been up to, and he knows I don't agree with the way he's raised you, and he brought you here anyway."

"Why would he bring me to you if he felt that way?"

"Maybe it means that some part of him realized he was going in the wrong direction, and he loved you enough to leave you behind."

"It would have been better if he stayed here, too."

"No doubt. But maybe, if we give him enough time, he'll figure that out for himself."

Blue stared at the ground. The morning was bright and growing hot, and the steady *tick-ticking* of the few remaining pinwheels in the garden competed with the birdsong.

Blue didn't know what to think anymore.

He was startled by the sound of Eve's hands clapping together just beside his ear.

"Time to get a move on," she said. "You're going to have to work faster than this if you want to set my garden back to rights, not to mention everything else you've got to repair today."

"I didn't break anything else!" Blue protested.

"You've got a friendship that needs mending, if I'm not mistaken," his grandmother said, grabbing his hands and pulling him up off the bucket.

She looked at the house. "And I've got a house full of relatives to deal with. Let me tell you, I can't wait to see the backs of them. It'll take the rest of the summer for us to put the place in order."

"What if . . ." Blue hesitated. "What if Ma Myrtle gives the new fate to the wrong person?"

"If you ask me," she said, "any person would be the wrong person. I've told Mama as much, but I'm not sure she'll listen."

"But, Granny Eve, your curse is so . . . if she would just tell you how to find Munch, you could have a new fate!"

She smiled at him. "Do you know I'm the best gardener in three counties?"

"I don't see—"

"Look at the size of that watermelon you skewered." She nodded toward a melon as big as a truck tire. It had a silver trophy stuck through it like a toothpick. "I was planning on taking that one to the fair. It looks like a heavyweight champion to me."

"I'm sor—"

"I can grow another," she said. "And when I do, I'll be proud of what it represents. My own hard work and skill. Not some talent spun out of the swamp by a power I don't properly understand."

"But your curse!"

"I'd erase it in a heartbeat if I could," she admitted. "But I wouldn't take a great fate in exchange for it."

"I would," Blue said fervently. "I would do anything for a new fate."

"I understand," she said. "Everybody feels their own way about this strangeness of ours."

Blue wasn't sure that was true. Most of the cursed Montgomerys seemed to feel exactly the same way he did.

"Maybe I'm different because I was wrong about my-self for so long." Eve looked thoughtful. "For all of those years, everyone assumed I had a talent for gardening."

"But then your husbands died," he whispered.

"Yes they did, and I loved them fiercely. And when I finally realized the curse was to blame, I was . . ."

Her eyes had gone damp. Blue looked away.

She cleared her throat. "Anyway, I didn't mean to start talking about myself. I've just been remembering lately. Back when I thought it was all a result of magic . . . well, back then I didn't enjoy gardening half as much as I do now."

THIRTY-FIVE

A REAL
HERO

Tumble and Blue met on the road, on their way to apologize to each other.

"You don't have anything to apologize for," Tumble said, kicking at the sand with the toe of her sneaker. "You didn't do anything wrong."

"I shouldn't have told you to leave. I should have listened to your explanation."

"About that . . ." she said. "Can we go for a walk? I don't want to talk about it in front of my parents, and Ida doesn't want me over at your house."

Blue thought about it. "I'm sure Ida will get over it. She doesn't seem like the kind of person who stays mad."

They walked down the dirt road, trying to stick to the spots where the pines shaded them from the heat of the sun.

"My parents brought me here because I couldn't stay

out of trouble," said Tumble. "And they don't even know about my fate. Blue, I'm not a hero. I'm a . . . I think I'm someone who needs saving all the time."

"No you're not," Blue said. That didn't sound like Tumble at all.

"Beast chasing me, the tree, the flare," she said, ticking incidents off on her fingers.

Blue frowned. "Those could've been accidents."

"Yeah, but I've been having *accidents* since I was a baby."

"What do you mean?"

Tumble took a deep breath. "I found out about a year ago," she said. "At one of my old schools we had to make family trees for an assignment. It was supposed to be a craft project. Our teacher said to be creative. I was painting mine on this huge roll of white paper, and I wanted it to be taller than I was."

"That's a big family tree."

"It would have been a piece of cake for you to do one that size," said Tumble. "But my family isn't like that. I mean . . . I only have one first cousin that I know of. So, I figured I was going to have to do a lot of research to find enough family members to make the tree look good."

"You could've asked your parents," said Blue.

"I did," said Tumble. "But even after they had named all of the relatives they could think of, the tree was still too short. I started looking around online for relatives, but instead of finding them, I found this article about my brother."

"You have a brother?" Blue wondered why she hadn't mentioned him before. "Where does he live?"

Tumble stopped walking. She reached into her pocket and pulled out a plastic snack bag. It held a short pencil, a pink eraser, and a ragged picture.

"Here," she said, passing it to Blue. "This is Jason."

The caption underneath the photo said, "Local Teen Remembered for Heroic Actions."

The boy in the picture did look like he could be Tumble's brother. Blue saw that they had the same nose, and the same square jaw. Jason was wearing a football jersey and holding a helmet under one arm.

"He died," Tumble said. "I was a baby."

Her voice was so odd, distant and whispery and not at all like the Tumble whom Blue had come to know.

He glanced up from the picture and saw that she was digging and digging at the dirt with the toe of her shoe.

"I knew he'd died, but my parents told me it was . . . they said he was sick. That he'd had a terrible asthma attack. But the article said that wasn't the whole story."

Blue didn't know if he should speak.

Tumble took a deep breath. "Jason was a real hero," she said. "Not like me. We didn't live in an RV back then. My parents had a house, and one night, there was a fire."

A chill trickled down Blue's back. "And Jason . . . ?"

"I think . . . it must have happened really fast. They couldn't get to me in my nursery. But Jason—he climbed up the side of the house to save me, Blue. He had to break the window to get me out. I guess we both breathed in a lot of smoke. But Jason's asthma . . . he didn't . . . he couldn't breathe."

Tumble rubbed at her eyes with the back of one hand.

"Tumble—"

"It was *my* fault!" said Tumble. "He was this wonderful, heroic person, and he died saving me. And I don't even . . . I can't even ask anything about it."

"Tumble," Blue said. "It's not your—"

"Like, did it hurt? Was he scared? I can't ever know, and I stay awake sometimes imagining—"

"It's not your fault."

"The worst part is that I owe him my whole entire life, Blue, and I can't do enough to ever make up for it. Now that I *know* I'm a damsel in distress . . . I wasn't worth it. How could I be?"

"You're worth a lot," Blue said in his fiercest voice.

"I can't even save someone from gerbils without barbecuing myself! And how would my parents have felt, if after everything Jason did for me, I died that way?"

"You're worth a lot to your parents," said Blue. "That's why they're here. And you're worth a lot to me."

"But, Blue, don't you get it? I can't help you," Tumble groaned. "I can't do anything right."

"I didn't want to be your friend because I thought you could save me," Blue said. "I wanted to be your friend because you *tried*. With the board games and the race. Even with the gerbils."

Tumble's hands were wringing the front of her shirt. "I ruined that. I know I did. Ida was doing fine, and I . . . I'm so sorry."

"You should probably apologize to Ida for that, not me."

"I will. And I have to apologize to Howard for his nose, and Millie, Jenna, your grandmother, even that Greg guy . . . it's my fault he doesn't have a tent to sleep in anymore."

"About Howard," said Blue. "We've got to figure out some way to help him. He's in serious trouble with this swamp cake thing. I'll explain later. But Greg's okay. He moved into someone's van."

"I'll apologize to all of them," Tumble promised. "It's the least I can do. The *only* thing I can do."

"*No*, it's not," Blue said. "Why do you keep saying—?"

"Because it's true!" Tumble cried. "This is why I've never told anyone! Because of course everyone will say I didn't do anything wrong, but it doesn't change the fact that I'm here and my brother's not."

Blue wondered what the right thing to say was. He couldn't imagine how hard it would be to feel like Tumble did.

"Is this why you're so obsessed with Maximal Star?" he asked as they started back down the road.

"I thought I could make it up to Jason." Tumble was

trailing behind him. "I thought if I was a hero, too . . ."

"Maybe there's some advice in the book?" Blue suggested. "Maybe he says something about how to help people even when you're accident-prone."

Tumble looked up. "You never finished that copy I gave you, did you?"

"I stopped just after Maximal saved that woman from the charging hippo."

"Oh, I love that part!" said Tumble, brightening a little. "It was so smart how he used the diaper pin."

"Um, yeah. It was interesting."

Tumble sighed. "Well, if you've read that far, then you know that Maximal isn't anything like me. He doesn't *ever* cause disasters. He only saves people from them. I wish . . . you know what I wish?"

"What?" Blue asked. He hoped it didn't involve hippos.

"I wish I could ask *him* how to fix my problem. If there was a way for someone like me to turn herself into a hero, he would know it. If I could just meet him, Blue!"

"Your parents still won't let you go?"

Tumble shook her head. "I haven't even asked. There's no way they would . . . unless . . ."

Blue looked back over his shoulder and saw her standing in the road, a familiar expression on her face. Tumble had a plan.

"What?" he asked.

"I'm supposed to be apologizing to you," said Tumble.

"You already did."

"No, I mean, I'm supposed to be *really* nice to you. My parents are glad that I have a friend."

"I'm glad to be your friend," said Blue. "What does that have to do with—?"

"If *you* were to invite me to go with you to meet Maximal Star, as a peace offering, it would be *so rude* of me to refuse."

She gave him a hopeful look.

"I guess," said Blue. "But who am I supposed to get to take us?"

THIRTY-SIX

TRYING IS
THE TRICK

B lue thought for sure it would never happen.

The Maximal Star event was scheduled for the day before the Grand Revue. And as the Revue approached, the Montgomerys were so frantic with plans, and Ma Myrtle was so demanding, and the house was so in danger of falling apart, that Blue felt certain his grandmother would change her mind.

A stage had been set up in the front yard. Cousin Greg was working on something he called a canapé cabana beside the garden. Ernestine's ukulele had been sabotaged. And Blue had seen two of his great-uncles unloading what looked like a red velvet throne from the back of a furniture truck.

The eve of Ma Myrtle's death was going to be more like a carnival than a funeral.

But somehow, even with all of that going on, Granny

Eve was sitting in her Thunderbird at exactly three o'clock. She was unwinding the rag rollers in her hair, and honking the horn for Blue to hurry up.

"We're going?" Blue asked as he slid into the backseat. "I thought with everything—"

"A team of mules couldn't drag me back into that house right now." She had put on makeup and a church dress. "We are going to eat food I didn't cook, and we are going to watch people who are not related to us put on a show. We are going to see what this Magnificent Starlight—"

"It's Maximal Star," said Blue.

"Honey, as long as he's not involved with the *Grand Revue*, he can be whoever he wants to be."

The Maximal Star event wasn't any less crazy than what was going on back in Murky Branch, but at least it was a different kind of crazy. The famous hero was supposed to be speaking at six o'clock in a high school gymnasium, but even though Tumble, Blue, and Eve arrived at the school more than an hour ahead of time, the parking lot was almost full.

Blue and Tumble sat on the Thunderbird's trunk, eating barbecue sandwiches and potato salad they had picked up on their way.

Tumble had only managed to take a few bites of her sandwich. It tasted good, but she was too busy staring toward the other side of the parking lot, where Maximal Star's tour bus was parked. Every inch of the bus was painted a glittering silver white so bright that the sun reflecting off it made her eyes ache.

Tumble couldn't believe she was this close to him.

People were milling around the bus, trying to see in, but women in tight silver vests and tall white boots were shooing them away.

"Who are they supposed to be?" Blue asked.

"Those are the Starlets," said Tumble. "You know, from the infomercials? I thought they were just for television, though. I didn't picture Maximal traveling with them. It must be kind of tough to do your heroing with that many people hanging around."

Almost everyone she could see was sporting Maximal Star T-shirts, buttons, or belt buckles. Many of them were carrying grocery bags, or even rolling carts, filled with copies of *How to Hero Every Day*.

"The line for the signing after the talk might be really long," Blue said.

"Don't worry." Tumble realized she was jouncing her legs up and down so that the whole car shook. She stopped. "I'm in the Young Heroes Fan Club. I have a card. The invitation said we're supposed to get VIP seating and first place in line if I show it at the door."

She had crammed her own copies of the book—a hardcover and three paperbacks—into her new emergency backpack. She'd made a point of not including any flares.

The backpack itself was one she'd used in second grade. It was bright pink and covered with daisies. Tumble was worried that daisies didn't send the most professional message, but it was the only bag she'd been able to find on short notice. No *true* Maximal Star fan would go to meet him without having her heroing supplies handy.

Looking around at the crowd, she couldn't help but think that none of them were quite like she'd expected a group of Maximal Star's readers to be. There were men and women in camouflage who arrived driving trucks with all-terrain tires and snorkels, like they were preparing for something apocalyptic. But there were also a lot of people wearing shoes they could never run in. Most of the purses Tumble saw were definitely too tiny for a proper first aid kit, and there was a lady wearing a long necklace made out of diaper pins. Which was interesting and all, but not the point. The worst were the ones wearing costumes—shiny tights and flowing capes—like they thought saving people was a joke.

And all of the kids Tumble saw seemed to be tagging along with parents.

Where were the other young heroes? Where were the other emergency backpacks?

For that matter, where were the acts of everyday heroism?

Not too far away, Tumble spotted an elderly man bending down to examine the tire on his Jeep. It had gone flat, but even though people were walking past him on their way to the tour bus or the booths that were selling collectibles and memorabilia, none of them offered to help.

Tumble didn't know how to change a flat tire, but surely one of those people driving the snorkel trucks did. She waited for someone to *aid and assist with alacrity*, but nobody did.

She passed her Styrofoam cup full of uneaten potato salad to Blue and hopped off the trunk. "I'll be right back."

When Tumble asked Maximal about how to be a hero even if fate was working against you, she wanted to be able to tell him that she hadn't given up. Maybe he would step out of his tour bus, and he would see her helping the man, and he would be able to give her advice.

Excuse me, young lady, he would say. (Tumble had always imagined that Maximal would be very polite.) *I see you don't know how to change a tire, but you're still doing your best. That is exceptionally heroic of you.*

And Tumble would say, *Listen, Mr. Star, I've got something to confess. I want to be a hero and save people, but I've got this huge problem.*

Oh? He would have a kind and understanding voice.

I'm cursed—please don't ask how, it's a long and complicated story—to be a damsel in distress.

Tumble didn't know what he would tell her to do, but she knew he would say something true and useful. Maximal Star had the best advice, and if anyone in the whole world could figure out how to help her, it was him.

She headed toward the old man and his Jeep, so lost in this hopeful fantasy that she didn't even see the minivan backing out of its parking space until she heard Blue shout.

"TUMBLE, MOVE!"

Blue had been following Tumble for exactly this reason. If you thought about it, which he had, a busy parking lot was basically one big obstacle course filled with rolling Tumble-squashers.

Instead of moving, Tumble froze, but the minivan's front windows were down, and the driver had heard Blue's shout. He hit the brakes.

"Hey, watch where you're walking!" he hollered.

"You watch where you're driving!" Blue hollered back. He grabbed Tumble's hand and tugged her out of the way. The driver threw a rude gesture out of the window as he sped away.

"What a jerk," said Blue. "Are you all right?"

"It's not his fault," Tumble said numbly. "It's me. I'm—"

"It's his fault for being mean about it," said Blue. "Most people would've stopped to make sure you were okay."

Tumble was looking toward the old man with the flat tire.

Blue followed her gaze and saw that he was standing up with a smile on his face. Whatever the problem had been, he must have figured it out.

Tumble sighed. "We've just *got* to talk to Maximal, Blue," she said. "Do you think . . . if we went up to the bus and explained things . . . would they let us in?"

Blue frowned at the Starlets in their silver uniforms. They seemed to be maintaining a perimeter around Maximal Star's bus, but what if there wasn't time for Tumble to ask her questions at the book signing?

"I guess we could try."

"That's right," Tumble said. "*Trying is the trick.* I thought you hadn't read that chapter."

"Um," said Blue, not wanting to disappoint her.

"We'll try until we make things change," she

announced, confidence seeping back into her voice.

Watching her walk toward the bus, straight-backed with her chin up, Blue shook his head. He wished he believed in something half as much as Tumble did Maximal Star. He didn't like their chances of getting in to see the man, but he figured he might as well do his part.

"Wait for me!" he called. "I'll watch for traffic!"

THIRTY-SEVEN

STARLETS

Amy the Starlet was friendly, but Blue thought it would have taken a tank to move her away from the door to Maximal Star's bus. She stood with her tall white boots spread shoulder-width apart and crossed her arms over her sparkly silver vest.

"Sorry, short stuff," she said, "but Mr. Star doesn't see fans until six o'clock, and it's not six yet."

"Not even Young Heroes?" Tumble asked desperately. She pulled her membership card out of her backpack and held it out to the Starlet.

Amy flipped the card over and squinted at it. "Oh, is this a kid's club thing? That's Lucy's job. She's over there."

She pointed to a booth where a Starlet with dark red lipstick and an Afro was selling coffee mugs, protein powder, and star-shaped key chains.

"It's not really a *kid's* club," Tumble said. "It's for heroes in training."

Amy the Starlet blinked so rapidly that the glitter on her eyelids dusted her cheeks.

"Come on," said Blue, hoping to stave off an argument. "Maybe Lucy can help us."

He tugged Tumble toward the booth. They had to wait in line behind a woman who was thinking about buying a Maximal Star Lantern. According to Lucy the Starlet, it was a flashlight "as bright as a shooting star."

"I'm looking for one with a fire-starter built in," the woman said.

"You could buy a Maximal Star Lighter, too," Lucy suggested.

The woman left without buying either.

"Typical," Lucy muttered.

Tumble cleared her throat, and the Starlet beamed at her. "Hi, there! You're *Maximally* decked out, aren't you? Is that your emergency backpack?"

Tumble's eyes lit. "Yes!" she said. "You could tell even with the daisies?"

"Of course!" said Lucy, nodding so that her dangly

earrings swung back and forth. "You look like someone who's *ever prepared for every eventuality.*"

"Oh my gosh!" Tumble squealed. "That's from Chapter Seven! I'm Tumble, and this is Blue."

Blue waved.

Lucy pumped her fists in the air. "Wow, you guys have even got heroing names! I used to call myself the Stinger when I was your age."

She made a lunging gesture, like she was holding an imaginary rapier. Then she frowned at Blue. "You don't look the part, though. You definitely need a T-shirt. Or a coffee mug. Do you like mugs?"

Were there people, Blue wondered, who had strong feelings either way about mugs? "I didn't bring any money."

"Oh, don't worry about that," Tumble said. "My mom gave me plenty for both of us. Pick something! Anything you want."

Blue didn't necessarily *want* any of it, but maybe buying something would put Lucy in a helpful mood. He scanned the objects, looking for one without a picture of Maximal's bright white smile on it. "Maybe the flashlight?"

"Great! Because it gets dark in your attic," said Tumble.

"Sure. Yeah."

"Not a big fan yet, is he?" Lucy said to Tumble. "But I can tell you're working hard on that." She pulled a boxed flashlight out from underneath the table in front of her and tucked it into a plastic bag.

"I'm going to convince him," Tumble agreed. "Or Mr. Star will convince him tonight at the talk. Do you think there will be time during the signing for us to ask him a question?"

"Well—"

"Right," Tumble said, snapping her fingers. "Of course not! Because all of these people are here to get their books signed. So, if a Young Hero had a *very important* question for Mr. Star, wouldn't it be better for her to see him before the show?"

Blue watched Lucy the Starlet's face. There was a brief hitch in her smile. "He's supposed to have a Q&A at the end of the talk. You'll be able to ask your question then."

"Um . . . but . . ." Tumble seemed a little flustered. "It's kind of a private question?"

"I'm really sorry," said Lucy, leaning over the table toward them. "We can't let fans in to see Mr. Star early. We're not allowed."

"Maybe we could—"

"I'm afraid not."

A line was forming behind them. Lucy handed Blue the bag that held the flashlight.

"Look," she said quietly, reaching out to take the money from a wilted Tumble. "I can't promise anything, but if you'll sit in the front, I'll try to sneak you backstage for a couple of minutes. We'll tell him you're a VIP. It'll be . . ." She glanced toward the tour bus. "Fun. It'll be fun."

Tumble perked up in an instant. "Really?" She grabbed Blue's arm. "Blue, did you hear that? I can't even . . . wow! Thank you so much!"

"Sure," said Lucy. "No problem."

Blue thought she looked awfully uncomfortable for someone who didn't have a problem, but Tumble didn't seem to notice.

"Seventy-five cents is your change," said Lucy the Starlet, holding three quarters out toward Tumble. "Stay heroic, you two."

THIRTY-EIGHT

MAXIMAL
STAR

There was no special seating for card-carrying members of the Young Heroes Fan Club, despite what the invitation had promised. But since Tumble and Blue were near the beginning of the line to enter the gymnasium, they managed to race to the front row ahead of the crowd.

Eve had said she'd find herself a place closer to the back since she didn't feel like running for it, so it was just the two of them. They sat on the edge of their metal folding chairs, waiting for some sign from Lucy the Starlet that they were allowed to go backstage.

The gym was still set up for what Tumble assumed had been a graduation ceremony. They sat a few yards away from a stage covered in potted ferns and heavy green bunting. The roar of the air-conditioning system was soon drowned out by the chatter of the crowd, who took their places in the rows behind them and in the stands to either side.

To the left of the stage, a Starlet was standing guard in front of a door. She kept trying to discreetly adjust one of her boots, never noticing how Tumble stared at her, willing her to wave them over or wink at them or do anything other than fiddle with the boot's zipper.

Would Maximal be carrying his own emergency backpack? she wondered. Or would one of the Starlets be in charge of carrying it for him since he was going to be busy speaking? Did he keep diaper pins on him all the time, like she did, and would he be willing to show Blue how useful they were?

She glanced at the time on her phone again. 5:55.

"Come on," she muttered. "Come on, come on."

"I bet Granny Eve wouldn't mind staying *after* the signing," Blue said. "She doesn't want to be around the house with all of the Grand Revue preparations going on anyway."

"I like your grandma," said Tumble, her eyes still fixed on the Starlet guarding the door. "I don't want her to be cursed. I don't want you to be cursed. I don't want an alligator to eat Howard. If Maximal can just give me a *little* advice, I know we can find a way to fix everything."

With two minutes to go before Maximal was supposed to appear, Tumble crashed her elbow into Blue's shoulder so hard that he swayed into the man sitting beside him.

"Sorry," he said hastily. "Tumble, what—"

"Lucy," she hissed, already halfway out of her chair.

The Starlet had poked her head out of the backstage door, and she was looking right at the two of them.

"Oh my gosh," Tumble said breathlessly as they followed the *clunk-clunk* sound of Lucy's boots down a hallway that smelled like fresh paint. "Oh my gosh. We're going to meet him. We really are."

Her eyes were so round Blue thought a surprise might make them roll right out of her head, and she was clutching her pink daisy backpack to her chest like it was the only solid thing in the world.

"I'm taking you to the green room," said Lucy. She cracked the piece of chewing gum in her mouth. "We're running a little late, but he should be there by now. You can ask him your question. Just be quick about it, okay?"

"Of course!" Tumble said. "I'll be so quick. Thank you so much."

"No problem." Lucy stopped in front of a classroom door. "We've got cookies and stuff. You can fix a plate if you want. Nobody will mind."

"Blue," Tumble breathed, "we're going to eat cookies with *Maximal Star.*"

Blue watched her walk into the room, so light on her feet that she seemed to be in danger of drifting away. He followed her inside and was disappointed to find that the "green room" was not green. It was just a classroom that had been turned into a staging area for Maximal and the Starlets. The teacher's desk had been filled with trays of cookies and energy bars and pitchers of ice water. The Starlets milled around chatting with other adults who Blue guessed were community representatives.

"He should be . . ." said Lucy, scanning the faces in the room. "Hang on, you two. Let me see if I can find out where he's gone."

She trotted over toward a Starlet who had on gold boots instead of white. Blue assumed she was the boss.

Tumble was still lost in her happy daze.

"Do you want food?" Blue asked.

"Do you think . . . would he mind if we took a picture with him?" she said.

"I think we should stay on track and ask him our questions first."

"Right. Of course. I wish my parents had come. If they could just meet him face-to-face . . ."

Lucy was on her way back to them already, and she was holding two star-shaped VIP badges that dangled from rhinestone-studded lanyards.

"So, we're definitely behind schedule," she said with an embarrassed laugh. "He's still on the bus. But I found these for you guys!"

Tumble had the lanyard around her neck almost before it was out of Lucy's hand. The VIP star hung right over the center of her chest and flashed in the classroom's fluorescent lighting.

"M'kay," said Lucy. "Why don't you have a seat and wait? I'm going to go get our promotional video playing for the people in the audience. I'll be right back."

Tumble and Blue sat at desks in the front corner of

the room, so that they would know the second Maximal Star entered. They waited.

And waited.

None of the Starlets or the other grown-ups seemed to care that they were there. Blue looked around. The Starlets also didn't seem worried that Maximal hadn't made an appearance yet. "What do you think's taking so long?" he asked Tumble.

She was staring at the door as if she could make her hero walk through it just by willing it to happen.

"Probably it's just an emergency," she said, as if emergencies were things that happened all the time. "Someone passed out from the heat, or he had a call from a person in crisis."

Fifteen minutes later, Blue was starting to think she was right. Tumble was too hyped up and distracted to make good conversation, so he'd been picking at the rhinestones on his lanyard. Whatever had been used to glue them in place was strong, but he'd managed to pry a few off before he noticed the boss Starlet watching him.

He was just wondering how annoyed his grandmother was getting, sitting in the gym waiting for Maximal to show up, when the door swung open and a scruffy-looking man slouched into the room. Even though he had the familiar spray-on orange tan and swishy haircut from his book cover, Blue wouldn't have recognized him if the Starlets hadn't all burst into action.

"You're not in your uniform!"

"Where's the mic? Did somebody fix it?"

"He can't go on like that. Not again."

"Coffee," Maximal Star grunted.

He looked like someone who'd just woken up and put on the first clothes he found. His faded shirt was stretched over his stomach, and his gray sweatpants belonged at a rummage sale, not on someone who was about to go speak to an audience full of fans.

"Coffee!" Maximal bellowed when the Starlets kept flitting around him like a swarm of flustered bees.

They scattered in every direction, except for the boss Starlet in her gold boots. She was trying to clip a small microphone to the neck of his shirt. She leaned forward to whisper in his ear, and he turned his bloodshot eyes toward Tumble and Blue.

■ ■ ■

It was him. Really him. Sort of. Tumble hovered halfway out of her desk.

"Maybe he was up all night saving people," Blue whispered encouragingly.

"Right," she said. "He probably was."

Of course he was, she told herself. This was Maximal Star, after all, and if he looked a little rougher and more bad-tempered than she had imagined, it was only because he had been working himself too hard.

She took a deep breath, picked up her backpack and walked toward him. She could feel Blue a step behind her, and she was grateful to have him guarding her back as most of the people in the room focused on them.

Shoulders back, head up—a heroic first impression. She was going to do this right.

"Mr. Star," she said in her clearest voice, "my name's Tumble Wilson, and I'm ready for any situation no matter how rough-and-tumble it gets."

The Starlet in the gold boots smiled and made an *awww* sound, but Tumble didn't let it ruin the moment. She could and would keep her head in any situation.

"I've read your book all the way through at least fourteen

times," said Tumble, "and I'm trying hard to follow the tenets of heroism. But I've got a big problem."

Maximal Star blinked at her. "Well," he said, and Tumble was relieved that he had the same deep, slow voice in real life that he did on his commercials. "Well, we can't have that. Tell me the problem, and we'll see what we can do about it."

Tumble wished other people weren't watching. If it were just her and Blue and Maximal, she could've explained how things *really* were, but she didn't want to talk about curses in front of everyone else.

"It's like this," she said, refusing to sound nervous. "Every time I try to save someone, I end up getting myself into more trouble than the person I'm trying to help. And then someone else has to come along and save *me*. It's almost like . . . like I'm jinxed or something."

Maximal yawned and scratched the back of his neck. "Are you *prepared with all of the proper precautions?*"

"Absolutely," said Tumble. "And I try to *preemptively plan for problems.* But everything still goes wrong. Do you . . . do you think anyone can be a hero? Even if they're up against something really tough?"

Maximal looked around the room. Everyone was waiting to hear what he said.

He flashed his white, white teeth and threw his arms out dramatically. "Of course anyone can be a hero!" he announced. "That's what the whole book is about."

"But if I always get into trouble—"

"Just stick to the tenets, and maybe try to start smaller. Little things are the way to go," Maximal said.

The Starlet who had refused to let them on the bus earlier approached with a cup of iced coffee; he snatched it from her and took a big sip from the straw. "See?" he said. "Amy here is my hero for fetching me this latte."

Several people laughed.

Tumble frowned. "I'm not talking about *coffee*," she said. "What if I need to do something bigger? What about all the people who need *real* help? What am I supposed to do about them?"

For the first time, Blue spoke up. "We're serious, sir," he said. "How is someone supposed to be a hero if they always end up in danger?"

"You two are cute," said Maximal. "Nobody expects a couple of kids to save the day. Leave that to the grown-ups."

Tumble's backpack slipped off of her shoulder and onto the floor. She didn't even try to catch it. "But in *How to Hero Every Day* you say—"

"Listen, I'm supposed to be onstage in a minute—"

"You were supposed to be onstage half an hour ago," said Blue.

Maximal kept talking over him. "So if you want me to sign your books or give you a photo op or something, now's the time."

Tumble looked down at her bag. This wasn't right. This was all wrong. "No," she said quietly. "No, I'm fine."

"Let's get you two back to your seats!" It was Lucy the Starlet, hurrying toward them.

"I'm fine," Tumble said again. "Completely fine."

Blue bent to pick up the backpack for her. "Tumble," he said. "We need to go back to the gym."

She frowned at him, but when he pointed toward Lucy, she turned obediently and followed the Starlet out of the room.

"You know it's not really a book for *children*," Maximal was saying as they left.

Blue slammed the door behind them.

• • •

Lucy talked too fast all the way back to the gym. "I've always thought that you couldn't be a hero at all if you didn't have something to struggle against. So if you're having a hard time, that's not necessarily a bad thing. Maybe you're training yourself up for something big and tough without even knowing it!"

"Uh-huh," Tumble mumbled. "Right."

"And . . . uh . . ." said Lucy, looking at Blue as if she was expecting him to step in. "You know . . . even wanting to help other people is pretty heroic. Most people are kind of selfish. So you're already a hero. In my books."

But Lucy's books weren't the ones that mattered.

As the Starlet's hand reached for the door to the gym, Tumble stopped moving. "I need some fresh air."

"Tumble?" said Blue.

She shook her head. "I need to go. I don't—I don't want my front row seat. Give it to somebody else."

"Are you—?"

She was already walking fast in the other direction, shoulders tucked in, head bent.

Definitely not ready for anything rough or tumble, thought Blue.

"*Oh*," said Lucy, watching her go. She lifted one hand to her silver vest as though she'd been stabbed in the heart.

"Your boss is an idiot," said Blue. "And I don't think he should be anyone's hero."

Lucy sagged against the door. "I'm so done with this job," she said. "I wanted to do something great, something fun and important! And instead everything's just crummy."

Blue knew what that was like.

THIRTY-NINE

A HAPPY ENDING

Blue found Tumble sitting on a bench under an oak tree outside the school. Even from a distance, he could tell who it was by the slump to her shape. Twigs and dried acorn caps crunched under his feet as he approached, but she didn't look up.

"Granny Eve will be out soon," he said. "I'm sure she'll figure out that we're not there."

"Okay."

Blue decided it was best not to notice if her voice was a little soupy.

He sat down beside her and handed her a fistful of money. "Lucy gave me a refund and let me keep the flashlight. She said it was the least she could do."

Tumble shoved the dollars into her pocket. "Great," she muttered. "I'm going to need to buy a new book to read."

Blue wondered what you were supposed to say to someone who'd just found out their hero was a fraud. Maybe there wasn't anything. Even if his dad showed up right now and apologized for everything he'd done, Blue would never feel quite the same way about him.

"I guess you think I'm pretty dumb, don't you?" said Tumble. "Crazy Lily Wilson with her crazy ideas about being a hero."

"I think Maximal Star is a selfish moron," said Blue.

"Yeah, but what does that make me?"

"It makes you an optimist." Blue hesitated. "Am I supposed to call you Lily now?"

She kicked an acorn cap. "I don't know," she said. "I wanted to be Tumble because Tumble could be a hero. And Lily was just some girl."

"I bet you weren't ever just some girl," said Blue. "Do you want to know my favorite thing about Tumble?"

She didn't answer.

"Tumble always believes there's a way to fix things. It's maybe the most impressive thing about her," he said. "Even when everyone else thinks something is impossible, Tumble's there saying, 'Maybe not. We have to try.'"

"How can *that* be your favorite thing about me? I've only ever made things worse. I almost roasted my-self. I let gerbils attack Ida. I got Millie Flat's heart broken. And unless Howard develops a sudden passion for swamp cakes, I may have ruined his life. Every-one will know he's been faking all this time, and he's going to be . . . the alligator is going to . . . it's so horrible."

She took a deep breath. "And on top of all that we didn't convince Ma Myrtle of anything, and there's only *one day* left before she chooses the Montgomery who gets to go into the swamp. What could we possibly do to fix it all in one day?"

Blue shrugged. "I don't know. *I'm* not very good at optimism."

Tumble fell quiet.

Blue looked around for something to comment on, but all he saw was one of the Starlets heading toward the tour bus with a clipboard.

"I guess you had the right idea days ago," he said at last, trying to make his voice light. "Someone really should go after that alligator and give it a kick in the tail."

Tumble huffed. "It would serve it right, cursing people for no good reason."

Blue nudged her with his shoulder. "You probably really *would* kick Munch if you met him. I'd be too scared that he'd come up with some worse fate for me."

Finally, Tumble smiled. "Maybe I would," she said. "But I think I'd rather ask him to uncurse both of us."

"You think that would work?"

"Well, it should be easier than giving us some great and wonderful fate, right? Just . . . ask him to undo all of it."

She looked up into the tree branches. The sky was dim overhead, but not yet dark. "The moon's supposed to be full tonight, right?"

"Yes," said Blue. "At least all of the relatives will be sleeping instead of running around with telescopes."

"Ma Myrtle's not even going to live long enough to see the red sickle moon."

Blue nodded. It made him sad. Ma Myrtle was difficult, but he couldn't imagine life at the Montgomery house without her.

"Maybe she's wrong about everything," he said. "Or

maybe she's just playing a trick on all of us. Maybe she'll live to be one hundred and spend her days laughing at everyone who fell for her prank."

"I'd like that," said Tumble. "That would be a happy ending."

It wouldn't really, Blue thought. So many things would still be wrong. But it was a very optimistic thing to say, a very *Tumble* thing to say, and he knew better than to argue with that.

Humans—always getting the story wrong in your own favor.

That monster Munch. That evil beast. Cursing children, eating them even. How could he? Why would he? What, oh what, shall we do?

Making it all about me. When the boogeyman has always been you.

Almira stabbed Walcott. Did I mention?

It was decades after we parted ways. She slipped the dagger in between the fifth and sixth rib, just shy of the heart. Why would she? How could she?

Don't you already know?

Her son was born with such a terrible fate. Tumble's fate, as coincidence would have it. Disaster struck the boy again and again, and Almira felt it every time as a blow to her own conscience.

Get rid of Montgomery, she thought. *As I should have that night. Fix it once and for all.*

Another curiosity of the human imagination—
this idea that you can un-break something. Piece
the fragments of shell together and put the egg
back in its nest if you like. What's inside will
never fly.

Walcott lived. Of course. Both of them lived
great, long lives, as they'd wanted. Healthy lives.
Wealthy lives.

They were given exactly what they chose for
themselves on that night, two hundred years ago
to the day, when they crossed the Okefenokee to
meet me under the impossible moon.

FORTY

IMPOSSIBLE MOON

The light was wrong on Tumble's face.

She was trying to sleep in her new bedroom, and like before, she was lying awake. She wanted to go out to the RV. She needed to.

But Tumble had decided that if she couldn't get anything else right lately, she could manage this one thing. She was going to spend the night in this bed, and then when it was over she would know that she had at least tried to do what her parents wanted. One night. She could give them that much.

Tumble lay there, hating the house more and more as the hours ticked by. Instead of letting her sleep, the house forced her to think . . . about Jason and Maximal Star and the Montgomerys. About how wrong she'd been at every turn this summer.

She was busy prodding these thoughts until they were

tender, so she didn't notice right away that the light had changed. It was pouring in through the window, spilling across her sheets, staining the white walls of the bedroom pink.

Pink?

It hadn't been earlier. With no curtains in the house, it was impossible not to notice the brightness when the moon was full. As it had been when Eve Montgomery drove her and Blue home that evening. As it had been when she climbed into bed not long after.

Tumble frowned, not yet curious enough to go look outside. Slowly, the pale pink light grew darker and darker, until the cream-colored quilt spread across the foot of the bed looked like it had been soaked in blood.

The box springs shrieked as Tumble rolled over. The rug under her bare feet was soft.

She went to the window and blinked out, realization settling over her like fog.

The whole night had gone that deep, dim bloody color. And the moon . . . she had to press her face against the glass and tilt her head to find it in the night sky.

The moon wasn't full anymore.

Tumble had traced the circle of it against the Thunderbird's window as Eve drove them home. It wasn't a circle now. She stared at it, not quite believing, but . . . hoping.

It was a red, red moon. It was a sharp, sharp sickle.

It was a chance when she'd been certain they'd run out of them.

Am I dreaming? she thought.

At that moment, a flash of white caught her eye. She squinted. Someone was coming up the dirt road toward the Wilsons' driveway. She might not have noticed him through the trees, but he was running with a twinklingly bright flashlight. The beam bounced up and down with the motion of his hand.

What do you know? thought Tumble. *It really does look like a shooting star.*

Maybe even the kind you could wish on.

She threw on her clothes. She grabbed her daisy backpack and filled it with everything she had collected over months and months of heroism training. Compass. Maps. Water bottles. Matches.

Who cared if Maximal Star wasn't what he'd claimed

to be? Some of his advice had to be good, and Tumble could use it for good. She would. She had to try.

She found Blue in the yard, tapping on the RV's door and shining his flashlight at the window.

When he spotted her he said, "It's impossible! I was having a nightmare, and when I woke up . . . But all of the relatives are asleep. None of them even suspect . . ."

And Tumble said, "We'll need a boat."

FORTY-ONE

THIEVES

They couldn't stop looking up. The moon was sharp as a blade, and it hung over them, so very red.

"It looks like a smile," said Blue.

"Maybe a cruel one," said Tumble.

She tripped over a tree root, and Blue grabbed the back of her backpack to steady her.

"My hero," Tumble muttered.

"Not for long," Blue said. "We're going to do like you said. We're going to tell Munch we don't need a great fate, we're going to ask him to uncurse us, and that'll be that."

The road through the woods to Goat's trailer was longer on foot, but it wasn't a hard trek. The frog song grew louder as they walked.

"I can't quite believe this is happening," said Tumble. "When I saw the red light—"

"I know," said Blue. "I was wide awake, but for a few seconds I thought it was a dream."

"Is it . . ." Tumble tried to think through what she wanted to say. "Does this all seem too easy? How can it be just me and you awake? How can it be tonight, right when we need it more than ever? After everything—"

"I think it was always going to be tonight," Blue said. "I realized when I saw the moon. There's a carving in Howard's bedroom, of Walcott pointing up at a circle. I think it's supposed to be a hint about the full moon turning into the sickle."

"So Ma Myrtle lied to everyone?"

"Maybe she doesn't know? Or she's got her own plans and the Revue is just a way to have fun and make sure the relatives don't leave before she dies."

Tumble was glad Myrtle Montgomery wasn't her great-grandmother.

A couple of minutes before they reached the trailer, they turned off the flashlight. "It's wrong, isn't it?" Tumble said, whispering despite the fact that Goat couldn't possibly hear them from inside. "To steal from him?"

Blue didn't answer right away. "But *everything* is

wrong," he murmured finally. "It's wrong for Granny Eve to lose people she loves. It's wrong that Howard has to lie to everybody so that they won't be afraid for him."

"And it's wrong that you can't win," said Tumble. "Everybody should be able to win sometimes."

"It's wrong that your heroing always backfires," said Blue. "If you weren't cursed, you could be a better hero than Maximal Star ever was."

Tumble didn't know if she believed that. But the idea that she would never get to try to be that hero, to make up for everything . . . that was the worst.

When they stepped out of the trees and into Goat's yard, it didn't take them long to spot the problem.

"Where's the canoe?" said Tumble. "It's supposed to be on the bank."

They searched the creek's sandy bank and checked the shed that held Goat's freezer, but the canoe was gone.

They stood on the bank, uncertain. This was supposed to be the easy part of their plan.

"I think . . ." Tumble hesitated. Maybe the canoe was somewhere obvious, and they'd just missed it? She squinted around, hoping to find it propped against a tree or lying near Beast's Dogloo. "I think I can work the jon boat's motor."

"You can?" Blue sounded impressed.

"It can't be that hard."

It took them a while to figure the boat out. Tumble found a long pole, and Blue took an old life jacket off of one of the posts on Goat's dock.

"This is better anyway," said Blue. "We'd wear ourselves out if we had to paddle into the swamp. Unless you can't remember how to get the motor started?"

"I can do it."

"Okay." Blue looked around for some way to help. "I can untie it. And switch on that light at the front."

"Good," said Tumble, bending over to continue her examination of the motor. "It might take us a minute to get going. It'll be loud. What if Goat hears?"

Blue swallowed. It wasn't Goat that worried him. The black water of the creek ran for miles, all the way into the swamp. And they didn't know the first thing about boats. Or navigating.

But if they didn't find the alligator . . .

Tumble must have been thinking the same thing. She said, "I guess we've tried everything else."

"Right."

They looked up at the moon.

"Should I steer?" said Blue.

Tumble shrugged. "Do you know how?"

FORTY-TWO

SPLASH

B lue did not know how to steer a boat.

Neither did Tumble.

Turning the motor was confusing. Left and right were backward, and even with the light mounted on the front, they nearly ran aground three times before they were out of sight of Goat's trailer.

Tumble wasn't sure she had angled the motor correctly. The nose of the jon boat seemed to be too far out of the water. She didn't know if that was her fault. Even if it was, she didn't know how to fix it.

"At least we're going forward!" Blue said over the engine's growl.

Tumble sat on the bench in front of him, holding the long pole and wearing the life jacket he had found. The jacket was dirty, and the straps were fraying. Tumble hoped it would still float in an emergency.

"You do know how to swim, don't you?" she asked Blue.

"Of course," said Blue. "Wait. You can swim, too, can't you?"

Tumble tried not to be annoyed at the sudden horror in his voice. He was only imagining all of the different ways she could die in a swamp, which was perfectly reasonable.

"Yes," said Tumble. "I was just wondering if I should give you the jacket."

"No," Blue said hastily. "No, no. You should definitely keep it. It looks good on you."

Other than the jacket and the pole, Tumble's backpack and the flashlight were their only supplies. Tumble was glad she had put the bug spray in the pack. Even with it on, they were both swatting a lot.

In places, the route ahead was so narrow and overgrown with vegetation that they thought for sure the boat wouldn't make it. Once, Tumble spied part of a fallen tree sticking up out of the water just in time for Blue to pull up the outboard. They slid over the tree, and thin limbs screeched against the bottom of the boat.

They barely made it. It was only with the help of the current, a lot of luck, and Tumble's well-timed use of the pole to push the boat off that they managed at all.

Unfortunately, Tumble put so much muscle into the task that she lost her balance and fell into the bottom of the boat, dropping the pole into the water. By the time she sorted herself out, they were drifting away from the tree, and the pole was out of reach.

"Maybe we won't need it again?" she said, trying to sound hopeful.

Soon, the creek narrowed in front of them, and Blue steered them carefully between the banks. The roots of the tall trees on either side were growing down toward the water like gnarled, grasping fingers.

Blue held his breath and concentrated, and then they were through, slipping between the tree roots and out of the creek entirely. The stream had taken them into a stiller body of water that opened up more and more until Tumble and Blue were gliding through an eerie landscape choked with lily pads.

Cypress trees bearded with Spanish moss surrounded

them. The moonlight stained the pale trunks red.

"Blue . . . if we follow the moon . . ."

It only took a moment for him to realize what she meant. The moon shone down from over the treetops. They would run aground.

"Maybe we're supposed to walk now," Tumble suggested.

Blue rubbed at a bite on the back of his neck, thinking. "What if we need the boat later? We can't carry it."

"We have to listen to the moon, right? Or they wouldn't have carved it into your attic."

Blue guessed that made as much sense as anything else, but there was another problem. "I'm not sure how to park the boat."

"Just drive it kind of slowly at land, I think. And don't get the propeller stuck in the mud."

"Okay," Blue said, wondering if he could manage that. "Let me know when we're getting really close to land."

Tumble nodded. She directed Blue through the cypress trees, following the moon.

"Wait," she said as a deeper darkness fell over them. "There's a cloud blocking it."

"The moon's not going anywhere," said Blue.

"I *know* that. But we need . . ." Tumble trailed off. Suddenly, she switched off the boat's light.

She knelt at the front of the jon boat, staring hard at the red-tinged water off to their right.

"What?" Blue said. Nerves were zinging through him. His grip tightened on the tiller. "It's not . . ."

He didn't realize he was expecting a giant alligator to pop up at any moment until it didn't happen.

"The water's red," Tumble said so quietly that Blue almost couldn't make the words out over the sound of the motor.

"Yeah, I know. Everything's kind of red."

She was excited now. She pointed. "It's a reflection of the moon!"

"So?"

"Blue," she said, annoyed. "There's a *cloud* over the moon, but *not* over the reflection."

"That's not . . ." *Possible*, he thought. But as he stared

into the water himself, he realized Tumble was right.

"The carving! That's why Almira was pointing down!" Tumble's voice echoed through the swamp. "We're *not* supposed to follow the moon. We're supposed to follow its reflection!"

The reflection wasn't perfectly clear against the water. It was more of a smear of gleaming red up ahead and to their right. As they pursued it, the lily pads parted in front of the boat's bow.

Tumble kept her eyes trained on the light. She felt better, more confident, since she'd figured out the moon's trick. It was a sign that they weren't wrong to be out here. They weren't crazy. They could make things better.

The glow led them steadily onward for a few minutes, before she noticed the change. "Are we going straight?" she asked.

"I'm trying!"

"No, I mean . . . I think it's moving."

They hadn't changed directions, so the reflection of

the moonlight against the water shouldn't have shifted. But it had. To the left.

"That way is all weeds and trees," Blue protested.

He wasn't wrong. Tumble could see where a cypress had fallen. Its broken trunk speared up out of the water.

"We'll get stuck," he said.

The red light was drifting ever more to the left.

"We have to follow it," Tumble said. "It's like a test of faith or something."

Blue took a deep breath, but he didn't argue. He turned the boat again. They were going to run through a huge raft of lily pads.

"The propeller," Blue said. "What if it gets tangled in those?"

Tumble didn't know. "Speed up?" she suggested. "That way we'll kind of mow through them?"

Blue had figured out how to go faster. The boat sped up.

"Faster than that!" said Tumble.

Suddenly they were zipping forward, toward the lily pads, then into them, the water behind them churning to a froth. They were doing it.

"Yeah!" Tumble shouted over the outboard's purr. "We're coming for you, Munch! Nothing can stop us!"

Something shrieked against the hull. The boat bucked under her feet.

And then it wasn't under her feet at all.

Tumble was in the air.

She was falling.

Splash.

FORTY-THREE

SURVIVAL PRIORITIES

Tumble bobbed like a cork. The water was thick with lily pads, and it was deep enough that she couldn't find the ground beneath her feet.

Move, she thought. *Move fast.* She kicked hard, trying to get out of the way of whatever was coming. Because there had to be something.

Whatever the swampish version of a curtain-eating dog or an exploding road flare was—it was bound to happen. She'd get tangled up in lily pads and drown. Or a snake would bite her on the ankle, and Blue would have to suck the venom out with his mouth, and then their friendship would never be the same because *gross.*

She kicked toward the boat.

"Blue!" she shouted. "Blue, are you all right?"

Blue had been thrown forward by the impact, but he

recovered quickly. "Don't come this way!" he shouted. "We're stuck on a tree or something."

Tumble stopped swimming a few feet from the boat. Blue was right. The water under the boat was probably full of sharp broken limbs. The last thing they needed was for her to be shish-kebabed in the middle of the swamp with no way to call an ambulance.

"But . . . can you turn the motor back on? Can you reverse?"

"Ummmm." Blue was staring down at Goat's boat.

"Blue?"

"I don't think I should try," he said at last.

"Well, you've got to! We've got an alligator to find!"

"Tumble, the boat . . ."

A mounting suspicion made Tumble's words come out high and nervous. "What's wrong?"

"The boat is kind of—just a little bit—broken." Blue was using what Maximal Star would have called an Un-alarming Voice.

Tumble was alarmed anyway. "Blue, is there a hole in the boat?!"

"Kind of."

"Kind of!"

"Yes," said Blue. "Yes, there's a hole in the boat."

"Are we sinking?"

"We're sinking."

"Blue!"

"But really slowly," he said.

They stared at each other for a long moment.

We're going to have to spend the night treading water in a swamp, thought Tumble.

We're going to die in a swamp trying to find a magic alligator, thought Blue.

The moon had reappeared overhead. It grinned bloodily down at them.

Tumble saw Blue pick up her backpack and put it on the bench in front of him to keep it dry.

"My phone's in there," she realized. She was still bobbing just out of reach. Her fingers were getting pruney. "Try to call someone."

They would be in so much trouble, but anything was better than floating here all night.

"You know we're not going to have a signal."

"So you're not even going to try? We're *stuck* in a *swamp* with a *sinking* boat!"

"Okay." Blue sighed. "But there's not going to be a signal."

He found Tumble's phone in the front pouch of the backpack. She saw the blue-white glow of the screen light up his face. *Work,* she thought. *Please work.*

"No reception," Blue said.

"Okay." Tumble tried to breathe deeply. "Okay . . . so what are we going to do?"

"I guess we have to swim," Blue said. "And then we walk back to the creek?"

Tumble was sure they could make it to land. They were surrounded by it, and it would be easy enough with the life jacket. But she wasn't certain about getting all the way back to the creek. And once they got there, how far would they have to walk to get back to Goat's?

"That sounds like a great plan," she said in the most upbeat tone she could manage.

■ ■ ■

Blue tried to keep his fingers from shaking as he rummaged through Tumble's backpack.

He found a bottle of water, a pocketknife, and a package of trail mix. His new flashlight was supposed to be waterproof, so he tied its strap around one of his belt loops and hoped for the best. He zipped the remaining supplies back into the pack and put it in the driest part of the boat he could find.

Getting into the water was tricky. He dropped the knife while he was easing himself out of the boat, and he only managed to hold on to the trail mix because he was clenching the bag between his teeth. But he had bigger problems to worry about. There were sharp limbs in the water, and Blue didn't want them to scratch his legs. Blood might attract alligators, and even if it didn't, he'd probably get some kind of swamp infection.

When he finally made it into the water, which was cool but not cold, all he could think about was the fact that he had not come prepared for swimming. His running shoes were weirdly buoyant on his feet, and the flashlight pulled at his shorts under the water. He paddled cautiously toward Tumble, one arm wrapped around the supplies.

She was fighting her way out of the life jacket.

"Don't do that!" Blue said. He ended up with a mouthful of water.

"We need to share it," said Tumble.

"No we don't!" he sputtered.

"You can't even keep your head above water!"

Blue had been planning on letting her carry the supplies since she had the jacket, but by the time he reached her, she had flattened it out on the water in front of her like a float.

"This isn't how you're supposed to use them," said Blue, reaching for the jacket.

Tumble snorted. "You're also not supposed to steal people's boats. Or drown in swamps. I think we're just going to have to ignore a few more rules tonight."

She tied one of the jacket's straps around the water bottle, but they ended up throwing the trail mix away.

"It's not like one package is going to do us any good if we're stuck out here," she pointed out. "Survival is about priorities."

They each kept a hand on half of the jacket to help them stay afloat as they kicked back the way they had come.

Tumble kept looking over her shoulder. Blue knew that the moon's reflection was still there, glistening red on the water.

"What if we were really close?" she said.

Blue, who had been thinking that reptiles probably loved hiding under lily pads, didn't know what she meant at first. Then, he caught the longing in her voice.

"No," he said. "No way."

"Blue—"

"Absolutely not," said Blue. "I'm tired. My bug spray is washing off, and I've inhaled at least three mosquitoes. We have one bottle of water and no food. And we've got no way to get back home before people realize we've been gone, unless we're extremely lucky."

He paused.

"And, Tumble, we're never lucky."

"I know that," said Tumble. "But maybe that means we don't have anything left to lose."

"Except our lives!"

"Now you're just being melodramatic. We'll be okay. I know how to build a campfire and everything."

Blue glared at her.

"Fine," she grumbled. "We'll keep going."

They kicked away from the moonlight. Toward home. And all of the things that were wrong there.

"But, Blue," Tumble said, "what if we were really, *really* close?"

"Tumble, *no*. We are *not* turning this life jacket around."

FORTY-FOUR

UPSIDE DOWN

"You're a bad influence," Blue said as they kicked steadily toward the moon's reflection. "And you're going to get us both eaten."

Tumble snorted. She was too breathless to laugh outright, but Blue heard her anyway.

"I don't think you should be allowed to giggle when you're swimming toward your death."

Tumble snorted again. "I'm laughing in the face of danger."

"Has that *ever* gone well for you?"

She decided not to answer that.

They had agreed not to swim so far that they couldn't see the boat anymore. At first, it had been difficult to keep their pace the same, and the life jacket had jerked to and fro as they swam, but they were finally falling into a rhythm.

Tumble was a little worried about how tired her legs were getting. It wasn't like swimming in a pool, where you spent half the time standing up in the shallow end.

They swam past a cypress tree, and the moon's reflection shifted farther to the left.

Blue was glancing back over his shoulder again. Tumble knew the dark outline of the boat must be almost invisible.

"We won't go much farther," she panted. "I promise. But we'll never forgive ourselves if we don't do everything we can."

They swam on.

Later, when they tried to describe what had happened, Tumble and Blue would never be able to recapture the strangeness of the moment.

They were swimming toward the moon's reflection. Something—she hoped it was only a lily pad stem—was wrapped around Tumble's leg, and she was kicking extra hard with that foot to knock it off. Blue was trying to hold the life jacket steady. Neither of them was paying as much attention as they should have been when the world turned upside down.

It happened all at once.

Suddenly, they were underwater.

Their hands were still gripping the life jacket, which was somehow below them in the water, and their feet were still kicking, but above them. They were swimming *down*.

Before Tumble could panic, before Blue could yell, the world flipped again, and they were jetting in the other direction. *Up, up.*

In an instant, Tumble's head and the life jacket broke the surface with a splash.

Blue came up beside her, sputtering and reaching for one of the jacket's straps.

"What happened?!" Tumble shouted.

"How did we get pulled under?!" Blue shouted back.

They clung to the life jacket together, their hearts pounding, their lungs demanding reassuring gulps of air.

Then they looked around.

They were still in the swamp but nowhere near where they had been.

Tumble and Blue were floating in a lake, bordered all around with tall grasses. The water was deeper here.

Even Blue's long legs couldn't reach the bottom before his head went under. And in front of them, a hundred or so yards away, was an island.

It was a small hummock of land rising above the still water, covered with tall pines and tupelos that stood out like inky columns in the darkness. A strip of muck and weeds ran along the side facing Tumble and Blue, and that narrow bank was covered in a writhing mass of scales.

Alligators—dozens of them.

They were lying there, row upon row, so that their dark prehistoric hides obscured most of the ground. In their midst, bigger than any of the others, was an alligator whose armor shone a burnished gold, even in the red moon's dim light.

FORTY-FIVE

UNDERWATER

"**M**unch," Tumble whispered. *"Don't move."*

Blue wasn't going to move. Or speak. Or think loud thoughts.

They held on to their life jacket, staring hard at Munch. He looked like a giant statue more than anything. No real alligator could be that big. It was difficult to make out the finer details in the darkness, but Blue thought his eyes were closed. They had to be closed.

Munch was sleeping, he told himself, and he was going to keep sleeping, and they were not going to be gator bait.

The moon was smiling right over the alligator's gleaming head, closer and bigger than it should have been, as if it wanted to remind them that this was what they had been looking for. This was their answer.

Blue hadn't expected the answer to appear so deadly.

He stared into Tumble's eyes, trying to communicate silently.

I don't know what to do, said her eyes.

We've made a terrible mistake, said his.

And she didn't disagree.

Each of them was waiting for the other's decision.

A sudden tremendous splash shattered the silence, and twenty yards away, between them and the island, a silver canoe rose out of the water. It was upside down, water sheeting from its sides, and someone was clinging to it with one arm.

The stranger struggled for a moment before he managed to flip the canoe. Then he brought his other arm up out of the water. He was holding a paddle. He tossed it into the canoe, and it hit the metal seat with a *BONNNG* so loud Blue could feel it in the water around him.

He stared at the alligators. They didn't seem to care about the clamor the newcomer was causing.

The stranger's face was covered by his wet hair, but he must have been able to see well enough because when he turned his head and spotted Munch, he had the same reaction as Tumble and Blue. He went still. For one breath. Two.

Then he dove under the water.

Blue stared at the place where he had disappeared. What was he doing? He couldn't hide underwater for long.

When the stranger's head finally popped up, he was farther away from them, closer to the island. He was swimming right toward Munch.

"Blue," said Tumble, panic stretching her voice thin. "Blue, he's going to beat us!"

Blue looked at the moon. He looked at the man swimming away from them, diving under again. He looked at the gators and Tumble and all of it.

This is a race, he realized.

And they were losing.

Tumble and Blue flailed with the life jacket for a couple of seconds before they both realized, at the same time, that they would be faster on their own. Tumble launched herself forward, and Blue went underwater.

He swept his arms in the smooth arcs he'd used so many times to cross hotel pools. He couldn't see under the water, so he caught what was happening around him in flashes when he came up for air.

Tumble was right in front of him for a while, and the man was a few yards ahead of them both. Then Blue went under. He kicked hard. Swept his arms.

And came up to find that he'd passed Tumble.

He went under again and moved forward through the water until his lungs hurt. When he broke the surface, he saw that he was gaining on the stranger, who didn't seem to realize yet that he was being followed.

He went under. Came up. He was still gaining.

But I can't win.

He could hear the deep thrum of Tumble's splashing legs and arms whenever he was underwater. She *could* win. Possibly. Only she wasn't a fast enough swimmer.

Blue thought of a new plan. He would catch up to the stranger, and he would grab on to him. Somehow, he would slow him down just enough for Tumble to pull ahead. He could do that much.

He swam as hard as he ever had.

Every time he went under the water, he pushed through it with all his might. He kicked until his sneakers slipped off and his legs throbbed. He surfaced for just long enough to gasp air, then went back down, not even checking to see how close he was getting to the other swimmer.

He couldn't afford to waste the time. Not until he was sure he was almost there.

When he thought he must be near his goal, he finally took a moment to look. It was hard to focus his vision. Lights were wriggling in front of his eyes, and he had a stitch in his side that tugged at him with every desperate breath.

The island was so close.

Blue could see the crimson gleam reflecting in Munch's eyes. The alligator definitely wasn't sleeping.

Was the stranger underwater? He must be almost to the shore. The thought filled Blue with a final rush of adrenaline.

I can't lose. Not again. Not this time.

He ducked his head and surged under the water as swiftly as if he'd been fitted with propellers.

■ ■ ■

Tumble was doing the perfect overhand stroke she'd practiced after reading about the time Maximal Star saved the crew of a yacht in Tahiti. But in the dark, with so few landmarks, she was having a hard time swimming in a straight line.

When she realized she was off course, she started looking up more frequently to get her bearings. That was how she saw everything.

The stranger and Blue were both under the surface when the golden alligator let out a booming bellow that echoed off the black water. Tumble didn't speak gator, but she knew a battle cry when she heard one.

The alligators reacted in an instant to their master's call. They slid into the water as one, an army of teeth and scales, and Tumble realized with horror that they must be aiming for the nearest intruder. The stranger's head popped up a few seconds later, but the alligators were already out of sight. He didn't know what was coming for him.

Tumble screamed. She was too out of breath for a good long one, and she didn't even bother with words.

She just screamed and gasped and screamed and gasped and slapped the water with both of her arms, trying to make as much sound as possible.

The stranger turned around.

Tumble took a deep breath. "The alligators!" she cried. "They're in the water!"

Whoever he was, he didn't need to be told twice. He started swimming toward her, arm over arm, water flying up around him as he flailed. Tumble treaded water, thinking fast. Blue was still under the water. But the stranger was making more noise so maybe Blue was safe.

Oh, she hoped Blue was safe.

Lines from *How to Hero Every Day* were running through her brain, but none of them told her what to do about an impending alligator attack. Maximal Star had never dealt with one.

All Tumble could think was that if she was going to battle with something that swam, she needed to get out of the water.

The canoe.

Tumble hated to do it, knowing the alligators were out there. But she took a deep breath and went underwater.

She wanted to swim quietly. Not loud like the stranger.

And I can hold my breath for a long time now.

She was up to seventy-nine seconds. If she got pulled under by strong jaws, that was how long she would have before she—

Swim, Tumble. Swim.

Her heart was trying to escape through her ribs. She kicked with everything she had left. When she surfaced, gasping, she was only a yard away from the canoe. It was floating low. She stroked toward it and saw that it was half full of water.

Tumble threw her arm and leg over the edge, bashing her knee hard against the metal side as she did. She tried to pull herself up, but the canoe tipped toward her, and more water flooded in.

No.

Tumble tried again. The wooden paddle slid out and splashed into the water beside her.

Tumble stopped. Her muscles were burning, and her arms were shaking. She wasn't going to be able to get into the canoe by herself.

She looked around for anything that might help and

saw the life jacket drifting nearby. She kicked for it, dragging the wooden paddle behind her with one hand. Suddenly everything that floated seemed important.

By the time she managed to struggle into the jacket, the stranger had reached her.

"Where are they? The alligators!?" He was wild-eyed and breathing even harder than Tumble, and he had strips of white medical tape across the bridge of his recently broken nose.

"Howard!"

"Tumble!" he shouted. "What are you doing out here?"

"What are *you* doing out here?! Blue and I saw the moon and we wanted—"

"Blue!" Howard whipped his arms, spinning around in the water to look for his cousin. "Blue! Where is he?"

Tumble saw him. He was at the island. He was climbing out of the water. *He's all right,* she thought. *Blue's okay.* Relief warmed her for all of a second.

Then Howard disappeared under the water.

FORTY-SIX

MEETING

Blue crawled onto the island, hands scrabbling at the weeds and roots along the bank to pull himself up. He'd lost his shoes during his swim, and one of his socks. He was hot, trembling, and light-headed, but he made it onto his feet. He stumbled forward, ready to grab—

Where had the stranger gone? Blue had to stop him from reaching Munch.

He felt the failure closing in on him. It was a wretched, familiar sensation. He'd tried. He'd given everything, but he still wasn't good enough.

Then he looked to his left. He saw the alligator. It was the old story come to life, only it was *more* than a story ever could be. Glowing and golden, the alligator watched him through slit-pupiled eyes.

The smile on its snout was wickeder than the moon above.

Tumble didn't think. There wasn't time.

Howard had gone down. Something—possibly one of the alligators—had dragged him under. She gripped the boat paddle in both hands and stabbed it into the water as hard as she could, aiming for the spot where Blue's cousin had disappeared.

If I hit him, so what? she thought. *So what? He's going to die!*

And maybe she would hit the alligator that had him instead.

She stabbed and stabbed until her arms screamed for her to stop.

Then she felt the paddle strike something fleshy and solid.

She didn't know if it was human or reptile or some other awful swamp monster, but she did know, right down to the bottom of her soul, that Howard Montgomery would rather be brained with a boat paddle than eaten alive.

So she jabbed the paddle down again, as hard as she could.

Some massive force under the water ripped it away from her. Tumble's wrist twisted, but she didn't even feel it.

There, just under the surface, was a pale hand, reaching for her help.

Tumble reached back.

Howard came up, coughing and spitting water.

"Are you hurt?" Tumble shouted in his face. She was still holding his hand in both of hers.

He grabbed for the shoulder of her life jacket. She went under for an instant, then bobbed back up as he let her go.

She spat out a mouthful of water. "I said ARE YOU HURT?!"

"I don't know!" Howard cried.

Tumble didn't believe a person could not know if his legs had been gnawed off. "CAN YOU MOVE YOUR LEGS?"

"Why are yelling at me?!"

Tumble paused. She hadn't realized that she was. She

took a few deep breaths. "If you can move your legs, we need to get to the canoe." She spoke in the calmest voice she could manage, which wasn't very.

Howard seemed confused.

"Swim that way!" Tumble commanded, pointing.

It was three kicks to the canoe, and then Howard held the boat still while Tumble rolled into it with a splash.

Tumble didn't think he would be able to get in, too. He was too heavy, and she was too small to balance the canoe while he climbed aboard. She yanked at the ties on her life jacket and pulled it over her head.

"Take it," she said, waving it over the side of the boat at Howard. "Put it on. And stop flailing around so much. You'll attract more alligators."

Howard's eyes were still bugging out of his head in a way that made Tumble doubt his ability to follow instructions.

"Put the jacket over your head," she said slowly. "It will make you float."

Howard splashed a lot more than Tumble would have liked, but he managed to get the jacket on.

He blinked up at her. "You saved me!"

Tumble heard the words, but at first they didn't make sense. She looked down at herself, safe in the boat. And at Howard, alive and wearing the life jacket. For now.

There was a *sploosh*, and Tumble saw the wooden paddle popping to the surface a couple of feet from the boat. Part of its handle was missing.

She clenched her jaw.

"We're not out of danger yet," she said. "But if you do exactly what I say, we will be soon."

Blue looked around, searching. An impossible realization was dawning on him.

Nobody else was here. It was just him. And Munch.

Blue was first.

What he felt then was magic. It was a happy, stunning sizzle. Somehow, he had made it to the island before anyone else.

He, Blue Montgomery, had *won*.

Unfortunately, his elation was brief.

From the water behind him, he heard splashing and Tumble's voice screaming. He whirled and spotted her, so much farther away than she should have been. She was slapping her arms up and down, sending up gouts of water that shone red in the moonlight.

"The alligators!" she yelled.

Blue looked around quickly, but all of the alligators that had been lying on the muddy bank with Munch were gone. He squinted into the trees, trying to see if they were hiding in the underbrush, waiting to lunge out if he drew near.

The splashing behind him grew louder.

A horrible thought struck like lightning. *Was Tumble being attacked?*

"Oh, I wouldn't worry about that," said a deep drawl of a voice. It was as slick as oil, and it was *right beside him*. "She's hardly a mouthful, that one. And the congregation wouldn't dare eat anyone tonight. Tonight's mine, after all."

Blue turned, slow and careful as you had to be with a predator.

The alligator wasn't there anymore.

Instead there was a man, too tall by half and dressed

all in dark gold scales. He had slit-pupiled eyes to match.

"Hello, Blue Montgomery," Munch said, stretching his mouth to show teeth like ice picks. "I've been waiting ever so long to meet you."

FORTY-SEVEN

MUNCH

Blue had things to say to Munch. And he would. Just as soon as his voice came back from wherever it had gone.

"Now," Munch said, pointing his smile toward the moon, "there are a few rules by which we must abide."

He held up a sharp-nailed thumb and a finger, pinched together, and a long, thin needle as bright as anything Blue had ever seen appeared between them. It looked like a sliver of starlight.

"What . . . ?"

"What did you think fate would be?" Munch held the needle out toward him. "*Now?* Or shall we wait for your friend?"

Blue stared.

"You're the first one here," said Munch. "Victorious at last. Congratulations. Felicitations. The choice is yours.

Do you take the night's fate? Or do we wait for Tumble Wilson?"

A big part of Blue was hungry. It wanted to reach out and grab the needle and change things, right that very second. But he and Tumble had an agreement. They had a plan.

"I'll wait," he said, rubbing his palms nervously against his wet shorts. "We've come to ask you for a favor. Sir."

"So *polite*." Munch's grin widened. "Of course we'll do what you say. You're the boss, Blue Montgomery."

Blue had never felt less in charge in his life.

"But you are," said Munch, his voice reaching deep into Blue's ears in a way that shouldn't have been possible. "I promise, you will never be more in charge of yourself than you are under this moon. No curse will hold you back tonight."

Blue couldn't stare into those eyes for long, but it only took a glance to see the darkness in them. And . . . the truth as well. What did it mean when someone had eyes that were both honest and evil?

"Don't worry too hard on it now," said Munch. He twisted the fate so that its sharp tip caught the red moon's light. "I doubt we will be meeting again after tonight. I tend to be a once in a lifetime event."

He turned his eyes toward the water.

Blue was almost frightened to look away from Munch, but he needed to know what was happening to Tumble. Something was going on back at the canoe. Tumble and the stranger were . . . together?

"Your companion is running behind schedule," Munch said. "And your cousin has reached the end of his courage. Time to speed things along."

There was a harsh, rumbling sound, and Blue realized with a swoop of fear that it was coming from Munch.

He took a step back, then hesitated. What if running away offended the alligator? The man? Blue was suddenly sure that Munch wasn't either. And he had the feeling that it wasn't smart to offend something you couldn't name.

He squinted out over the water. Tumble was paddling the canoe slowly toward them, and then she was moving fast. Faster than anyone could paddle. Even Goat's jon boat hadn't moved that quickly.

Tumble skimmed across the water toward the island, and Blue saw the stranger clinging to the side of the canoe. He was getting closer. He looked terrified. He looked like . . .

"Howard!" Blue called.

Tumble's own face was startled but not frightened. Blue assumed that was because she didn't realize what was propelling the canoe. He could see them now behind her—dark tails cutting through the water. And to either side of the boat, shining eyes appeared just above the surface.

"Good boys," Munch murmured.

The canoe slid ashore, hissing across the weeds and throwing Tumble backward. She rolled out of the boat and ran around to the other side to check on Howard.

Blue hurried to help.

Howard was lying facedown in the mud, either too frightened or too unconscious to move. Whichever it was, Blue didn't blame him a bit.

But even in the bloody light, Tumble looked as alive as Blue had ever seen her. She pressed her fingers to Howard's neck to check his pulse, and then she beamed up at him.

"I did it!" she said, her voice euphoric. "He's passed out, I think. But I saved him!"

"Tumble, listen—"

"Blue, you don't get it. *I* saved him. And nothing went wrong! I didn't get hurt, just normal bumps and bruises. *I* saved *him*. And *nobody* saved *me*."

"Great," said Blue, "that's great. But, Tumble. The alligator. I think you should know—"

"Where is he?" Tumble said, determination taking over every inch of her body. "Where's Munch? We're going to get what we came for, Blue! Even if I have to turn that alligator into *boots*."

Blue gulped. "About the alligator," he whispered. "He's not exactly an alligator."

"Huh?"

And then Munch was there, quick and quiet as a slither.

"And here she is," he said, smiling his pointed smile. "Fresh as a lily flower and every inch the hero of the story. Hello, Tumble. Blue insisted that we wait for you."

Tumble took a single step back. "Is this . . . ?" she said, staring from the golden man to Blue and back again. "Are you . . . ?"

"At your service," Munch said, his voice sleek. He glanced up at the moon. "For at least a few more minutes."

For the first time, Blue realized that the night was getting brighter. The red was draining slowly from the moon, which had fallen lower in the sky.

Munch held out his hand so that Tumble could see the needle. The glitter of it reflected in her wide brown eyes.

She recovered much more quickly than Blue had. "We're here to ask you to uncurse us," she said, her voice direct. "If you don't mind, Mr. Munch."

"I don't mind at all, Tumble," he said. "Just prick your finger—any one of them will do—against the night's fate. A drop of blood seals the contract. And it's done. And more than done."

"What does that mean?" Blue asked. It couldn't be that easy. Munch didn't seem like the kind of creature who dealt in easy solutions. "'More than done?'"

"I'm not able to 'uncurse' you any more than I was able to bless Almira. Or Walcott. I'm not a wizard, children, and I'm certainly no angel. I have only one trick, and that is to be here on the red moon night offering *this* to whomever chooses it."

He looked at the needle. The fate.

"Lovely, isn't it?" he said. "Every human dream in

one tidy little package. Touch it, and the world is yours. Fame, fortune. Fetching features if you care about such things. You've both tried so hard to get here, and now, all you have to do is lift a finger one last time, and you'll never have to try again."

Tumble's eyebrows drew low.

Blue guessed what she was thinking. "That's not how it is, though," he said. "Even for all of my relatives who have talents. I mean, my dad has one of the best ones, but he doesn't have *everything* he wants."

Tumble nodded. Her mother could fix things, but that didn't mean her life had been picture perfect wonderful like Munch was describing.

Munch shook his head. "Such a shame how the power has been misused. You mustn't take the present state of things as an example. Almira and Walcott were afraid to get their hands dirty. They hadn't the fortitude to do as they should have. And they didn't have the foresight to realize they would come to regret their cowardice.

"They chose to break the needle in two. I warned them, of course, about the consequences. They lost most of the power of it, and what they managed to keep was . . . tainted."

There was a pause while Tumble and Blue unraveled the story.

"Well, Blue and I aren't going to fight each other to the death, if that's what you're suggesting," Tumble said finally.

"Of course not," said Munch. "You two are friends. I'm sure proceedings will be much more civilized tonight."

Blue blinked. "So . . . are you just going to give it to us? The fate?"

Munch held it out to him again. "Here it is."

The point of the needle was so sharp. Blue imagined that pricking your finger on it would hardly hurt at all. He took a deep breath and reached out with a trembling hand.

Munch pulled it back. "Of course, as soon as it touches blood it disappears."

Blue, his hand still outstretched, stared at him.

"What?"

"Into the blood," Munch said casually. "It's intravenous. It changes you from the inside out. How else would it spread down through the generations? Oh, your children and grandchildren will thank you for what you're doing tonight, Blue."

Blue looked back at Tumble. Her hair was so wet that it had to be dripping into her eyes, but she was staring at Munch without blinking.

"But we're *together*," said Blue. "We're not like our ancestors. We helped each other get here."

"That's right," Tumble said quickly. "We don't need some big, life-changing, great fate. We just want to be normal."

She looked to Blue for confirmation.

He nodded. He had to admit that what Munch was talking about—a life where everything went your way, every day, without you having to suffer even a little for it—sounded like a dream. But he could do without that.

Just as long as he could wake up every morning with the *possibility* of that victorious feeling he'd experienced tonight.

"Oh, I'm *sorry*," Munch said, drawling the last word until it was almost a purr. "But deep down, you must both have known that tonight was a race for power. And that's just not a team sport."

Hello again. I suppose you're wondering.

Man? Alligator?

Silly human labels, and besides that, it's not really your business. Tumble and Blue certainly never found out.

How I wish you could have seen them. Gaping like I'd snatched a fish from their jaws. It was Montgomery and LaFayette all over again.

Humans . . . so predictable. Generations pass. Eons. The clothes change. The superstitions shift. You fiddle new baubles and gizmos into existence. But look deeper, and it's always the same with you.

I never see anything new.

Of course Tumble and Blue were friends instead of enemies, but I've always known that the line between liking and hating is thin as a reed. One can turn so swiftly into the other.

And when it did, how could anyone blame them? Tumble and Blue needed what I was offering.

Not *wanted*, mind you, not like their ancestors. Almira and Walcott could have changed their lives any number of ways. It was just that spending a few hours in a swamp filled with deadly dangerous creatures was the easiest option.

Make no mistake, I *am* the easy option. If you believe otherwise, you are a fool, and I do hope to meet you one red night.

But Tumble and Blue—they had to stand before me, side by side, knowing that they had found the exit and it was only wide enough for one to pass through. Perhaps, if they had never had that taste of success, it would have been an easy matter.

If Blue had never known that winning was as good as he'd always suspected it might be. If Tumble hadn't known the strength and joy of saving herself.

But I made sure they knew.

Do you think me cruel?

It really doesn't matter, but I'm curious.

I would argue that I am only what I ever have been. Fair.

It's my job to offer a choice, and a choice is what I offer. One free of doubt or misunderstanding. I opened their eyes so that they could make the decision with knowledge of what they would be gaining. Or losing.

And then I left it up to them.

FORTY-EIGHT

CHOICE

Tumble and Blue stood with their backs to the water's edge, facing Munch and his needle and his choice.

Tumble thought he looked as smug as anyone she'd ever seen, and she hated him with a hatred that withered her inside until she felt mean and small and not like herself at all.

As for Blue, he couldn't even see Munch's face. His vision swam. He didn't know if it was dizziness or tears. He only knew that Tumble deserved to be happy as much as he did.

More even. All she wanted was to help people.

But he couldn't quite bring himself to say what he knew he should. *You take it*, he thought. *Take it and get it over with quick, Tumble.*

He just had to accept losing one more time, so that

he could lose every time until he died. He squeezed his eyes shut.

"Tumble," he said, dragging her name out from between his teeth. "You should—"

"Shut up!" she said, her own voice choked. "You shut your mouth right now!"

Tumble wanted to scream. She knew who deserved a great fate, and it wasn't her.

Blue was kind and brave, and he only wanted to win so that he could be closer to his father. Tumble had been trying to save people, sure, but not *for* them. At least not entirely.

She'd wanted . . . to feel better. To erase all the guilt that kept trying to drown her. And she hadn't even managed that much. She wondered if Jason's picture had survived the swim through the swamp in its plastic bag.

All of those *x*'s. Were they still waiting for her?

Am I even a good person deep down? Suddenly, Tumble didn't know.

The red was paling. The night had turned a deep pink

that reminded Tumble of raw meat. They were almost out of time.

Munch stood before them as patient as a snake sunning himself on a rock.

Tumble opened her mouth. Maybe she would never have the chance to make the right decision again without causing herself disaster, but tonight, just this once, she could do it. She would. "Blue, you take—"

"*No,*" Blue moaned. "No, I can't."

He reached for her hand.

"Tumble," he said earnestly, "if you take it, you might actually do something amazing with it. How many people could you save? You would be *more* than a hero. You would be a superhero. A real one. That's . . . that's not me. Even with the fate, that's not what I would do. It will be better for *everyone* if you do it."

That's true, said a little voice inside of Tumble. *You could make up for everything. And more. You could help so many people. You could even rescue people like your brother.*

With a good fate running through her veins instead of a bad one, who knew what she could accomplish? Forget the *x*'s, Tumble Wilson might save the whole world.

Her free hand lifted toward the needle. Then lowered. She only wished she could be sure that the wet on Blue's face was swamp water.

She looked around for someone or something to tell her what was right, and her eyes landed on Howard's unconscious form.

He must have seen the moon just like we did, she thought. *And he knew it was his only chance to save himself from . . .*

Relief swept through her. Here was a decision she couldn't avoid. The choice wasn't hard to make after all.

"Howard needs it," she said to Munch. "Way more than either of us. So that you don't ever, you know, *eat* him."

Beside her, Blue felt the pressure on him drop.

Yes, of course. He was horrible for not thinking of it himself. He and Tumble could probably survive for ages with their fates, but poor Howard was definitely going to die a terrible death one day. Maybe even tonight.

Blue stared at Munch's ice-pick teeth. "Give it to Howard. I agree with Tumble."

Munch lifted scaly brows and glanced toward Blue's cousin. "Such thoughtful humans," he said, "but I'm afraid the night has taken its toll on dear Howard. He's not awake."

"So?" Tumble said angrily. "Just give him a jab with the fate anyway."

"He won't mind," Blue added.

"Being unconscious disqualifies him," Munch said. "This is about *choice*, and he can't make one."

"Well, wake him up!" said Blue.

"You just want to eat him!" Tumble accused.

Munch was sucking on his teeth and frowning. "I would rather not, to be honest," he said. "He's been consuming those dreadful swamp cakes to excess. And I usually prefer a nice fat bass fish, but I will admit that I can be . . . less than discerning when the moon's power wanes."

Blue gagged and slapped his hand over his mouth to hold back anything worse.

Tumble felt ill herself.

Munch shrugged one shoulder. "If it eases your mind at all, I imagine he will be much older by the time we cross paths again."

Blue's mind was not eased.

Munch looked at him. "You needn't be so alarmed. My other form is quite formidable. I'm sure I can manage the job in a single bite."

Blue sat down hard in the muck. He stared at his legs sprawled out in front of him. He wondered how they had given up like that without his permission. His remaining sock looked almost white in the moonlight.

It was time, and there was only one choice.

"Tumble," he said. "Take the fate. Prick your finger, and become a hero. I'll be fine. You can save Howard and everyone else who needs it."

Tumble narrowed her eyes at Munch. "Would that work? If I took the needle, could I save Howard?"

"Sorry," said Munch. "His death has been set. And I believe you two have already discovered that you can't play fate against herself. She doesn't like it."

Tumble braced her feet in the sand.

"It seems to me," Munch said, "that Blue is *choosing* to let you have the power."

He glanced at Blue, and Blue nodded.

"And if you choose to take it, then you can save people, if you wish. Wealth, strength, intelligence, charisma—all yours. What couldn't you accomplish with such resources at your disposal?"

Tumble looked down at Blue. He struggled to his feet. If Munch was going to make them do this, he wanted Tumble to know he was with her all the way. "It's the right thing to do," he said. "I want you to have it. You're a good person. You deserve it."

Tumble looked into Blue's eyes, and saw that he meant it. He thought she was a good person, that she could be a hero. Even after everything. He believed it.

Seeing that belief . . . for the first time in her life, Tumble knew it was true. She *could* be a hero. She could help.

Her goal was just one drop of blood away.

"We'll be friends no matter what," she said, reaching out to hold his hand again, "won't we, Blue?"

"Even if you're the most famous person in the whole

world," Blue said, squeezing her fingers tight. "If you still want to be my friend, I'll be yours."

"I'll always want to be your friend."

He smiled. A real smile. His hand was warm in hers.

Tumble steadied herself with a breath. "Give me that needle."

"The choice is made," Munch said formally. He tipped his head, and passed the fate to her.

For a few seconds, Tumble marveled at the needle.

She had to. It was cold and heavy in her hand, and she could *feel* the power. It buzzed against her fingertips like someone had bottled all the potential in the world into this one small decision.

Such a tiny, enormous thing.

And it was hers. She took a deep, deep breath. The choice, as Munch said, had been made.

Tumble brought her other hand up fast, and felt the needle bite into flesh. Too hard. Munch had said you only needed a prick, and Tumble had delivered something that was more of a stab.

But the blood welled. The needle dissolved into star-light.

And Blue was too shocked to cry out from the pain.

He looked at his hand, still trapped in Tumble's. The place between his thumb and forefinger, where she'd stabbed him, was pouring blood down both of their clasped hands.

"Tumble," he gasped. "What did you do?"

"My mom always says the choice you're making right now is the only one that matters." She let his hand go. "Maximal Star may not be a hero in real life, but *I* am. And this is my choice."

Munch hissed. He was staring at them, one hand raised as if he had wanted to stop Tumble but hadn't been quick enough. His pupils had contracted until they were nothing but razor-thin lines breaking the gold of his eyes.

"What happens now?" Blue asked him. "Am I still cursed? The choice . . . I chose for Tumble to have it. But she chose . . ."

Light flashed in the sky overhead.

Tumble and Blue looked up just in time to see the

moon go white. It righted itself in an instant, no longer a smile, but a fat full moon.

When they turned back to Munch, the man was gone, and the tail of a huge golden alligator was disappearing into the palmettos.

You Are Cordially Invited To

The Montgomery Family's

GRAND
REVUE

A FUN-FILLED FESTIVITY IN HONOR
OF OUR BELOVED MATRIARCH

MYRTLE MONTGOMERY

Featuring:

Artwork • butter churning • darts •
eating contest (swamp cakes to be pro-
vided by Flat's Restaurant) • fireworks •
gerbils • honky-tonk • ice-cube carving •
• juicing • kickboxing • a memorial
musical (inspired by Ma Myrtle herself) •
needlepoint • poetry • quilting bee •
races (three-legged and relay) • soccer •
• timpani • ukulele • victuals and
waterslide.

Tumble and Blue didn't know how far they were from home. Perhaps Munch's island was days away, or perhaps it was right around some corner that only existed when the alligator wanted it to.

"Murky Branch is on the western edge of the swamp," said Tumble.

Blue shook his head. "I'm not sure which way—"

She pointed confidently. If they paddled that way for long enough, they would have to make it out eventually.

They flipped the canoe over to empty it of water, and after a brief search under the trees, Blue found a thick, flat piece of bark that he hoped would work as a paddle.

"What about the alligators?" he asked.

Tumble was hunched over Howard, splashing water

on his face. "Let's not go swimming this time."

Blue helped her tighten the life jacket straps around Howard's chest before they heaved him into the canoe. He didn't budge, not even when they accidentally let his broken nose drag through the mud.

"It's . . . a little possible . . . ," Tumble panted, "that I hit him in the head . . . with a boat paddle."

Blue pulled the Maximal Star flashlight off his belt loop and shined it at Howard's face. "He doesn't look bruised or anything," he decided. "Maybe tonight was too much for him. It must have taken a lot for him to come out here, knowing that he might be eaten. And then to be pulled down . . ."

They arranged Howard so that his head dangled over the front of the canoe's middle seat and his legs over the back. He looked like a lumpy wet blanket that had been hung out to dry.

Tumble climbed into the front of the boat, and then, with a strong push from behind, Blue slid its nose out into the water.

"Careful," said Tumble. She held on to the sides of

the canoe and tried to balance while Blue placed his foot cautiously over the rear seat.

Blue's bark paddle was too delicate to help them off the bank, so the two of them had to scoot back and forth in their seats to slowly jostle the canoe away from Munch's shore and into the dark water. Ripples undulated outward from the hull to mar the still surface.

It was so quiet now, Tumble realized. Even the frogs were silent as she with her broken paddle and Blue with his piece of bark sent the canoe skimming slowly west.

She looked over her shoulder. Munch's island seemed lonely without its golden resident on the bank.

"We did it better than they did," said Tumble.

"Almira and Walcott?" Blue thought about it. He and Tumble didn't know what they had done. If the choice was what mattered, then did the fact that they had made two different ones change things? Or was the great fate Blue's now, hiding somewhere under his skin?

All he knew for sure was that they hadn't betrayed themselves, and they hadn't betrayed each other.

"Yes, we did," he said. "We did it way better than those two."

He dug his makeshift paddle into the water. Once, twice. Then, for the second time that night, up was down.

Down was up.

The whole canoe plunged underwater, and Tumble and Blue held on tight.

When it was over, they bobbed, wet and sputtering, in the creek. They were only yards away from the pale sandy bank beside Goat Flat's dock.

Blue stopped flailing when he realized his feet reached the bottom. He stood, holding on to the overturned canoe with one hand to keep it from drifting away on the current. When he looked around, he saw Tumble. She was already tugging Howard to shore by the straps of the life jacket.

A minute later, she and Blue were pulling the canoe out of the water.

"Do you feel any more powerful?" she asked.

Blue set Goat's broken paddle beside the canoe, then he lifted his hand and squinted at it. The place where Tumble had pierced him with the needle was sore, but there wasn't much to see. Especially not in the grayness of oncoming morning. The blood had washed off, and it was just a pinprick of a scab now.

"Not powerful," he said. "But different."

Tumble leaned toward him. "Lucky?" she asked hopefully.

"I don't know about that," said Blue. "I feel . . . like no matter what happens next, we're already through the hardest part. I don't think it's fate I'm feeling—good *or* bad. It's just me. I feel better about me."

Tumble tilted her head. "I get it," she said finally. "I feel like I'm stronger because of tonight. I didn't need Maximal Star when it came down to it. I made my own decisions."

"You gave up the fate," Blue said quietly.

"And you tried to give it to me." She bent in half to check Howard's pulse again. "It's just what friends do."

Blue insisted that Tumble let him and Howard confess to stealing Goat's canoe and wrecking his jon boat.

"That's not fair!" she protested. "I'll go with you! I'll help you explain."

"It's not about what's fair. It's about what's best." Blue rubbed his sore hand. "You already did a lot for me tonight, and this is something I can do for you."

"But—"

"You need to talk to your mom and dad," said Blue. "It's time to tell them you know the truth. And that will be a lot harder to do if they're yelling at you."

He's right, thought Tumble. But still . . . she couldn't let someone else accept her punishment for her.

"It's not like Howard and I will be in *more* trouble without you," he pointed out. "And at least my family won't think we've lost our minds, chasing after an alligator in the middle of the night."

It was hard to argue with that. Tumble took Blue's flashlight and set out for home on her own.

Blue waited until she had disappeared into the trees. Then, his one wet sock squishing with every step, he headed for Goat's trailer. He had to knock a few times before Goat, wearing just an undershirt and boxers, answered the door.

"Blue?" He yawned. "What—?"

Blue didn't know what he looked like, but he guessed from the way Goat's eyes suddenly goggled that he looked like a boy who'd just crawled out of the swamp.

"I broke your boat," he said. He was too drained to feel afraid of Goat's reaction. "The jon boat, I mean. Howard's down by the canoe. We went into the swamp. It was a Montgomery thing. We didn't mean—"

"Howard?" Goat asked, looking around for Blue's cousin.

"He won't wake up."

Goat pushed past Blue and ran toward the creek.

Several minutes later, when Eve Montgomery's Thunderbird soared out of the trees with its headlights blazing, he still hadn't asked Blue a single question about the missing boat.

"Munch wasn't exactly an alligator," Blue tried to explain to his grandmother. "And I gave the fate up, but then I got stabbed with it anyway. I'm not sure what that means."

Howard was lying behind them in the backseat of the car, finally awake. "Alligators," he groaned. "Alligators *everywhere*. It was the worst."

Eve gripped the steering wheel as if she wanted to wring the Thunderbird's neck.

Apparently, Ma Myrtle *had* told someone everything she knew.

She'd told Eve a few days ago and revealed that the

whole Grand Revue was a ruse. Like Blue and his cousins, Ma Myrtle had wanted her daughter to have the change of fate. She had planned everything to make sure the relatives were too busy and exhausted to guess the red moon's secret.

But, as she'd told Blue that morning in the garden, Eve didn't want a great fate. She didn't trust the magic, and she didn't trust the alligator. And so she had been playing along until the night passed in the hopes that no one would make the trip into the swamp and risk another disaster like the one Walcott and Almira had wrought.

"All of this deceit and insanity and croquet mallets flying out windows!" She was breathing so hard through her nose that Blue thought she sounded like a dragon about to snort flame. "And then you two, my *own* grandchildren, go tearing off into the Okefenokee by yourselves! You could have *died*!"

"Sorry," said Blue.

"Incredibly sorry," said Howard.

"I'm putting you both in bed the second we get home,"

their grandmother snapped. "And I'll glue you to the sheets to keep you there if I have to. Don't think I won't!"

Tumble's parents were awake by the time she finished her shower. She could hear the gurgle of the coffeepot through the house's thin walls.

She examined herself in the bathroom mirror. Her face was paler than it should have been, but her starry blue bathrobe covered most of the scratches on her arms and legs. One of her wrists ached, but it wasn't swollen.

She picked a clump of moss off the top of the shower drain, stuffed it into a paper cup for camouflage, and then tucked it into the trash can. It would be hard to explain random bits of swamp vegetation on top of everything else.

She put antiseptic on her scratches. She brushed out her wet hair.

Too soon, everything was done. Tumble didn't have any more excuses left.

She padded into the kitchen. It smelled like coffee. There was a place set for her at the table. A glass of orange juice, toast, and a boiled egg.

"Morning, sweetie," said her dad. "Ready for the big day? I'm looking forward to the poetry contest myself. Do you think they'll only let Montgomerys enter?"

"I got the toaster working while you were at the Maximal Star speech yesterday," her mom said, gesturing to Tumble's plate with her coffee mug. "How about that?"

Tumble sat down. It had been a whole lifetime ago that she'd met Maximal Star. She drank her juice in three quick gulps, then wiped her mouth on the sleeve of her robe. The fluorescent light droned overhead.

Tumble took a deep breath. She could have held it for seventy-nine seconds, but she didn't.

"Why didn't you tell me Jason was a hero?" she asked. "Why didn't you tell me that he died saving my life?"

B y eleven o'clock that morning, most of Murky Branch had turned out for the Grand Revue.

The sun shone in a cloudless sky, and for once, it wasn't unbearably hot. There was a buffet brunch on the lawn, courtesy of the Flats, who had closed their restaurant for the day so that every member of the family could defend their honor in the eating contest.

With the exception of Millie. She sat outside of Howard's bedroom door for hours, holding a brand-new box of MoonPies in her lap and snapping at anyone who made too much noise going up and down the stairs.

Blue found her there when he came down from his attic after a too-brief sleep.

"What if he doesn't wake up in time for the competition?" Millie asked. "Mrs. Eve said he needed to rest, but it's been so long—"

"He hit his head last night," said Blue. "Maybe he shouldn't be doing something that strenuous anyway."

Millie's eyes widened. "He hit his head? He can't compete if he's injured!"

"It wouldn't be fair," Blue agreed.

"But I told Daddy that Howard was going to give him a run for his money."

"It'll work out," said Blue.

"How do you know?"

He shrugged. "I'm giving optimism a try."

He really was.

That was why he stopped in the front entryway before heading out to join the festivities. The answering machine, miraculously undamaged after weeks of Montgomery mayhem, was on a small table beside the staircase.

It was blinking red with a new message.

Blue pressed the button.

Even though he'd been hoping, he was still surprised when his dad's voice came over the line. He sounded less casual than usual.

"This is Alan. Things are taking longer than I thought."

Breathing. "But I'm getting everything lined up for another season of racing." A nervous cough. "I was thinking maybe Blue could stay with you on into the fall."

Blue closed his eyes.

"If he wants."

Blue waited for the disappointment to come. It did.

But part of him was glad that he would be here with Tumble and his cousins when school started.

"Tell him . . . of course he can call if he needs anything."

Blue had told him what that was already. But he was starting to realize that what he needed was something his dad didn't have to give.

The answering machine *beebeeped*.

That was the end of it.

And Blue had a Grand Revue to attend.

Outside, things were in full swing.

Blue found a group of kids and the Okra Lane Seniors in the middle of a round of musical chairs. There were layer cakes for prizes, set up on a table in the center of the circle. The music stopped and everyone scrambled to reach a chair. Mrs. Lane was left on the outside of the ring.

"And I wanted one of Goat's Italian cream cakes so badly I could taste it," she said with a sigh as she walked over to stand with Blue. "Have you seen your great-grandmother? We came to visit her, but I can't seem to find her."

"I'm sure she'll be here soon," Blue said.

He wasn't, actually. Ma Myrtle had finally decided to make time for the Montgomery who mattered most. She and Eve had left in the Thunderbird as soon as Blue's grandmother had finished helping Howard up to his room.

Blue hoped that wherever they were, they were eating food Granny Eve hadn't cooked and watching people who weren't related to them put on a show.

He searched the crowd for Goat and eventually found him in the backyard cheering for the twins, who were passing a baton back and forth in the relay race.

Jenna and Ida didn't know yet that the red sickle moon had come and gone, and they were still trying to stay ahead of the other Montgomerys however they could.

Goat told Blue that the two of them had dominated at ice-cube carving, but that they had suffered a crushing defeat during the butter churning speed round.

"Three-legged race is next," he said. "You'd think they would have an advantage in that one."

"I'm so sorry about your boat," said Blue. "It was wrong of me to take it. I'll pay you back somehow. I'll clean a thousand fish for you if you want."

Goat shook his head. "I'm just glad y'all are all right. Your granny already wrote me a check for the boat. And for the broken paddle—can't imagine what you boys did to it. But it's her you'll need to pay back."

Blue nodded. He owed Granny Eve for so much more than that.

It wasn't long before Goat wandered off to check on the other Flats, but Blue wasn't alone for long. Tumble appeared at his elbow as if his thoughts had summoned her.

She was wearing a gray T-shirt without a trace of Maximal Star anywhere on it.

"I just got here with my dad. He's already trying to

take control of the poetry contest over by the chicken coop," said Tumble. She rolled her eyes. "The lady who's judging told him she doesn't believe in off-rhyme."

"Did you get a chance to sleep?"

Tumble shook her head. "We've been too busy talking."

They watched the twins finish the relay and cheered loudly when they came in second place behind two cousins from New Zealand. The victors were given a trophy that Blue recognized at once.

"That's the ballerina from my attic!"

Ida, who was stumbling past on her way to one of the watercoolers, paused. "Granny Eve said it was time to recycle those old trophies," she said. "She said that you'd need the space if you wanted to keep living in the attic after everyone leaves. Jenna and I won matching tiaras earlier."

"Twenty minutes until entries are due for the three-legged race!" Marisol, the cousin who was prone to car accidents, was dressed in referee's stripes and leaning on one crutch while she bellowed into a megaphone. "No latecomers!"

When the invitations for the Grand Revue had first gone out, Blue had briefly imagined that his dad might show up. He had thought about how perfect it would be if he made it in time for the three-legged race.

Opposites. Back when they still thought that would work, Blue had fantasized about crossing the finish line with his dad. Arm in arm. Both of them winners.

Knowing it wasn't going to be like that, at least not anytime soon, hurt. But not so much that Blue couldn't stand it.

"Do you . . . want to enter?" Tumble asked him. "Together?"

Blue rubbed the spot where the needle had gone into his hand. "I'm not sure *that* much has changed," he warned her.

"I'll enter us anyway," she said. "We have to have changed something. You can't go to so much trouble and come out with nothing. You just can't."

Optimism, Blue thought as he watched his friend march off.

He reminded himself that he'd made it to the Murky

Branch sign faster than he ever had before. Just the other night. It wasn't twelve minutes, but Blue wasn't his dad. And he didn't want to be.

Maybe he and Tumble had broken a curse. Or two. Maybe they'd done something bigger than that. But even if they'd only wasted a great fate, it had been their decisions that mattered, and Blue thought they had made good ones. It was time to find out what happened next.

He hurried back to the house to get a new pair of running shoes.

Howard's were floating around somewhere in the heart of the Okefenokee Swamp.

Monica Wilson was late to arrive at the Grand Revue.

She'd needed time to herself after the talk they'd had at the breakfast table that morning. Her Jason would have been so proud, she thought, of the girl his little sister had become.

She spotted her daughter and Blue taking their positions in the starting lineup for the three-legged race. She hurried over to cheer Lily on.

A small crowd had gathered to watch the race. When Monica tried to work her way to the front of it, she bumped into someone and almost lost her balance. How she had failed to see the man, she couldn't imagine. He was head and shoulders taller than every other person in sight.

"I'm sorry," she said. "I wasn't paying attention."

At least, she reasoned, she must not have been.

Nobody who was paying attention could have missed this fellow. He was wearing a strange suit made of scaled gold leather, and he had on a pair of those contact lenses with the slit pupils that she had seen before on Halloween. It was a wonder everyone in the crowd wasn't staring at him.

"Are you a relative?" Monica asked.

"Friend of the family," said the man, giving her a thin-lipped smile that never showed his teeth. He had a sleek, dark voice.

"Oh, us too!" said Mrs. Wilson. "That's my daughter about to start the race."

She pointed at Lily and Blue.

"Charming girl, I'm sure," he said.

The referee blew her whistle, and the racers hobbled off. Lily was laughing as she and Blue staggered forward.

"They're taking the lead!" Monica cried. "Go, Lily! You can do it!"

"Do you think," the man said in that curious voice of his, "that they're going to win?"

"They just might," said Monica, pumping a fist in the air. "Look at them go!"

While she cheered, the golden man watched the race with narrowed eyes. "Wouldn't that be interesting," he murmured to himself. "Wouldn't that be something new?"

END

A FEW MORE WORDS

Before I became an author, I had no idea how many people are involved in turning stories into finished books. For you readers who wonder about such things, I'd like to introduce a few folks.

Elena Giovinazzo is my literary agent. She's the one who sells my books to publishers. She reads my stories and helps me decide when they're ready to meet the world. She's a true friend, and I don't know where I would be without her.

Namrata Tripathi is my editor at Dial, which is an imprint of Penguin Random House. She edited my first book, *Circus Mirandus*, and together we turned *Tumble & Blue* into a story I'm proud to share. Nami is smart, patient, and bold. She convinced me I couldn't let go of this alligator tale, and she helped me revise it until I got it right.

Kate Beasley is my sister. She's an author, too, and I dedicated this book to her. That's only fair because I make her read every word I write. And I write a lot of words.

These three help me to be the best writer I can be.

When the writing is mostly done, there are people—so many of them—who make the book look its best and help it find its way into the hands of readers. Designers, copy editors, marketers, artists, publicists, and others—I'm sorry I can't mention everyone by name, but you should know these people are out there. They're the ones who make the books we read, and I'm so grateful to them.

One more thing before I go.

You won't find Murky Branch on any maps. Nor will you find Munch's island or the route Tumble and Blue take to reach it. But you *will* find the Okefenokee Swamp. It's a special place, and despite a certain alligator's opinion, visitors are welcome there.

Thank you for reading this story. Never forget that you're the hero of your own.